Reviews

"…a very special blend of warmth & wit." ~*RT Bookclub*

"…full of everything indicative of her personal style and flair. There are loveable characters that come to life, a charming storyline, and an abundance of the humor one has come to associate with Holly Jacobs' books." ~Kelley Hartsell, Love Romances

"…a trip worth taking to leave you smiling and feeling good." ~Carol Carter, Romance Reviews Today

"Holly Jacobs works her magic again…" ~Sharon Wren, Women on Writing

"Ms. Jacobs does a fabulous job describing the personalities, foibles, and follies of small town living. Zoe and Mace have a wonderful chemistry, and their dialogue is sharp and witty. Ms. Jacob's characters are funny, fresh, and make you want to sit down and chat with them a while." ~ Cat Cody, Romance Junkies

"I highly recommend…for someone looking for a little laughter." ~ Marlene Breakfield, Escape to Romance

"…a wonderfully funny story." ~Lydia Funneman, Writers Unlimited Reviewer

THE MAKEOVER

HOLLY JACOBS

Ilex Books 2019
ISBN: **978-1-948311-01-4**

Originally published as The Hundred-Year Itch by Harlequin Books

CHAPTER ONE

"*Hiho, Ohio, a quiet, lovely town. Hiho, Ohio, where no one wears a frown…*"

Zoe Wallace grimaced.

The fact that Hiho, Ohio's name made comedians within a hundred mile radius happy, was one thing. But the fact that the official town song was enough to make dogs howl was another thing. A terrible thing.

The song was horrible. Worse than nails on a chalkboard.

Oh, the singers were enthusiastic and even close to being on key, but even Pavarotti would be hard-pressed to make this particular song sound good. As a matter of fact, the only way it did sound good was when it wasn't being played.

Zoe had yet to meet a towns-person who liked the song, but she'd never met one who wouldn't defend it or the town's name to any outsider who dared mock them.

It was sort of like having a relative you didn't particularly care for but would defend in a New York minute if anyone else dared to put them down.

Zoe realized the chorus was silent and watching her expectantly. As chairperson of Hiho's Centennial Festival it was her duty to encourage the chorus. She forced a smile and clapped. "Excellent. Just excellent, everyone."

The director beamed. "And from there, we thought we'd sing a birthday song. After all, it's not every day your town turns one hundred."

The chorus started singing again and a voice behind her said, "*Psst*, Zoe."

She turned and saw Bertram Barky hiding in the shadows behind one of the auditorium's columns.

Bertram used to work for her aunt at Hiho's weekly newspaper, The Herald. At seventy-something, he had long since retired, but he still liked to pass on juicy tidbits to Zoe, who he'd adopted as a surrogate granddaughter when she took over the paper.

Oh, sometimes those tidbits were more gossip than news, but they were always interesting.

She smiled. "Hey, Bertram. What's up?"

"Sh," he said, a finger pressed against his lips. "Come with me. We can't talk here. Someone might overhear us."

"But I'm in the middle—"

"It's important. The biggest scandal to rock Hiho since Tabitha Carter from the bar ran off with Pastor Mitch." Bertram was pulling at her arm. "Come on."

Zoe gave the chorus a wave, not interrupting their singing, and allowed Bertram to pull her out of the Middle School auditorium into the bright May sunshine.

"Now, what is it?" she asked when the big door to the auditorium slammed shut behind them.

"Not here, someone may see us. They'll try to stop me. They don't want me talking to you or anyone from out of town. Come on."

Bertram often had tips, but he'd never played this cloak-and-dagger kind of game before.

Not knowing what else to do, Zoe followed him into the alley at the side of the building. "Okay, spill it."

"Its all a lie," Bertram said, excitement evident in his voice.

"A lie? What's a lie?"

"The whole thing. The Centennial."

Zoe shook her head. "I'm not following you."

"Hiho, Ohio isn't one hundred years old this month."

"It's not?"

"No."

He waited, and finally Zoe asked, "So how old is it?"

"Ninety-nine."

"Are you sure? Everything I've read indicates that the town is one hundred this year. Hiram and Hortense Hump filed the papers early in 1918. It was official May 1918. It's on our charter."

"But what you haven't heard is that something went wrong." He pulled a small notebook out of his pocket and consulted it. "Hiram told the town the paperwork was approved, but really, they had to refile everything and the town wasn't official until February of 1919."

"Well, that's interesting, but still I don't think it warrants this spy treatment."

"Don't you see?" he asked. "They want to keep it quiet."

"Who are *they*?"

"They. The Mayor. The Chamber of Commerce. Everyone. You have to break the story in the Herald."

"This is just hearsay, Bertram. You know that. That fire fifty years ago destroyed almost all the official documents. The town's Charter says May 1918. So, as far as anyone is concerned, 1918 it is."

Bertram looked as if he was going to argue, but Zoe held up her hand. "Let's say you're right. Let's say it really was 1919, not 1918. It's just not that big of a deal. I mean, if we'd known, I'm sure we'd have put off the Centennial Celebration until next year, but still—"

"It is a big deal if we want that Pawley Family Endowment. The terms were it was to be awarded to the college and the library *on our centennial*. If it's not our centennial, they'll pull it and the college has already broken ground on the new building. It's borrowed against that money. But the news is the news. Tell me you're not going to let them cover this up. This is big, Zoe. I held the proof in my hand. A letter from the newspaper's archive, but they took it and *lost* it and—"

"Uncle Bertram, there you are," Pete Matthews, Bertram's nephew, said as he headed down the alley. "Alice has had me looking for you for almost half an hour."

"See, they're trying to keep me away from reporters, even you," Bertram whispered to Zoe as Pete approached.

"Come on, Bertram, it's time to go home. Alice has dinner waiting on you."

He practically pulled Bertram out of the alley and down the street.

"Pete, wait a minute, I'd like to ask you some questions—"

"Later, okay, Zoe? I've got to run. You know Alice, if I don't get back she'll have my hide."

Zoe did know Alice Matthews, and Pete was right, she ran their restaurant and their family with an iron fist... tempered by a loving heart and some of the best food in the state.

"I'll catch you later then, Pete," Zoe said.

"Zoe, don't you forget what I said. The truth is out there," Bertram called as Pete practically dragged him down the street.

Zoe felt an old familiar burning in her stomach. When she first started working in New York she thought the sensation was the mark of a good reporter who sensed a story.

Now she knew it was an old ulcer flaring up, something that rarely happened since she moved to Hiho.

She didn't want a big story—she didn't want a scandal. She'd like to sweep the Centennial issue under the rug and ignore it, but she couldn't just let it lie. She'd have to check this whole thing out. It would be like having an elephant under a carpet—as much as she tried to ignore it, she'd know it was there, wiggling just beneath the surface.

Great. Another item on her list of things to do.

As coordinator of the Centennial Festival, the list was already long and only getting longer. The first events started in a week and there were still hundreds of details to attend to.

Zoe pulled out her list and scribbled *Bertram* at the bottom.

As she wrote it down, she saw what headed her list for tomorrow and groaned. There, in black and white it said, *Thelma Jean.*

Oh, how could she have forgotten? Probably a mental block. She'd promised Thelma Jean from the Snip and Clip, she'd get made over.

Not that she wanted a makeover. She sort of liked her look as it was. Easy to maintain. Comfortable.

But Thelma Jean was giving away a makeover as a prize at the Centennial Festival and wanted to take some digital photos of Zoe's before and after, then distribute them at the festival in a flyer.

Zoe had felt as if she had to say yes. But she had a feeling she wasn't going to like it.

Not like it at all.

"…and this is Mace Mason, here at WMAC News, where nice news matters."

Theodore Mason—Mace to his friends and fans—felt as if he were practically shouting. It was hard, even with a microphone, to be heard over the wails of the baby he was holding.

"And cut," the cameraman said.

As if he were playing the childhood game, hot potato, Mace handed the crying infant to its anxious mom and put down the mic.

He turned to the cameraman, "I think that's a wrap."

"Great story, Mace," Kip said.

Mace didn't even bother to answer the man. *Not that he didn't like Kip, but Great story, Mace?*

The story was sap.

Pure sentimental drivel.

Mother of triplets at home with a second unexpected batch of triplets…that wasn't news. His assignment editor wanted to use it for a Mother's Day tribute. *A Montage of Moms*, she was calling it.

She thought it was a great idea.

Mace thought it was bleck. Pure and simple drivel.

He was a reporter. Not that anyone would know it from the stories he covered for WMAC. How was he ever going to jump to a bigger, harder-hitting station if they kept giving him these fluff pieces?

He made quick work of the drive back across Erie, Pennsylvania to the office, ready to head to his small cubbyhole of a cubicle, when Stephanie Cooper, his assignment editor, snagged him.

"Mace, come on back here," she called.

Mace reluctantly headed into her much-larger-than-a-cubby-hole office.

"Sit down, Mace."

He'd have preferred standing so he could make a quick get-away, but he sat. Stephanie was the boss, despite the fact that the stations hallmark motto was her idea, Mace liked her…most of the time.

Today, after spending almost an hour with triplet infants and their triplet toddler siblings, wasn't one of those times.

"I have a new assignment for you," she said happily.

Too happily.

Mace was suspicious whenever an editor seemed this pleased with an assignment.

"I still have to edit that triplet piece," he said cautiously.

She waved the comment aside. "You'll have time. I want you to leave tomorrow on assignment."

"You're sending me out of town?" Hope surged to life.

He'd always dreamed of going out on assignment. Foreign countries, world hot spots. He wasn't talking about a quick trip to Edinboro, Pennsylvania but something out of state.

The short-lived hope popped like a bubble. Somehow he didn't think foreign locales were what Stephanie had in mind.

"I've got a new idea for Erie Chronicles," she continued.

Chronicles was Mace's baby. Mini-documentaries on the town's rich history. He'd found that digging into local legends and personalities fascinated him. So far he'd done eight half hour episodes and hoped to do more. It was his favorite part of the job. Chronicles was the reason he was still here at WMAC.

They tied clips from the show into the news program and the viewers' and, more importantly the advertisers', responses had been good.

"And the idea is?" he asked, cautiously.

"Hiram Hump."

"Pardon me?"

"He was cursed with a horrible name, but went on to do great things. He wrote *Erie, a History* back in 1896, before moving. That book is considered a priceless jewel of our city's history. There's a first edition at the library on display. They even have a statue of him. Hiram moved to, and founded, Hiho, Ohio, which gives us a bond to the town. This is their Centennial. I want you to cover it. Collect some bits on Hiram's years in Ohio, and cover their Centennial Celebration. We'll use some pieces on the news now, and use the others for the next Chronicle. Spend the week and relax. Think of it as combining work with a small vacation."

"What do you mean by relax?" he asked suspiciously.

"I mean, you're tense and irritable. Everyone at the station has noticed." Stephanie sighed. "Mace, you're a great reporter. You have a great eye for gathering unrelated bits of information and putting the pieces together in a relatable way, which is why your Chronicle series has taken off. We're lucky to have you. But you're not happy. I don't know if it's the job or something personal, but you need to fix it. Your attitude is interfering with your work."

"I'm a professional. Nothing interferes with my work," he said between gritted teeth.

"You're terse with the staff and they've noticed. I've had complaints."

Granted, he wasn't as sunny as *Pollyanna* Paige Montgomery, who gave the term *chipper* a new standard to live up to. Her terminal good mood was even worse since her marriage.

He might not be Pollyanna Paige, but he wasn't mean.

No, not mean. Terse. That's what Stephanie said.

"Who says I'm terse?" he asked.

8

"It doesn't matter. What matters is you're going to cover the Hiho Centennial. You leave tomorrow and will be there for the entire week, right through the firework finale."

He was going to find out who thought he was terse. Not that he'd do anything to them. No he wouldn't do anything accept kill them with sweetness. He'd be so sappy and gooey with it that even Paige would look *terse* next to him. And his target would probably overdose on pleasantness.

Visions of vengeful niceness danced through his head as he asked, "Are you sending a camera man?"

"No. You'll do your own camera work."

This wouldn't be the first time he'd done his own camera work. Mace prided himself at being a jack-of-all-trades. He shot a lot of his own footage for Chronicles.

"And while you're putting together this piece," Stephanie said, her voice serious, "I want you to think about what it is you want. You're valued here, but I don't know if WMAC is where you want to be. You have options."

"I—"

"We'll talk when you get back," she said, the conversation obviously over.

Mace left the office. He was going to Hiho, Ohio.

What a horrible name for a town.

He had a feeling this was going to be the longest week ever.

Mace mentally reviewed his notes as he pulled up in front of The General Store on Main Street, Hiho, Ohio, late the next afternoon.

Hiho, Ohio. Population 15,000. Named after *Hi*ram and his wife *Ho*rtense.

Hiho.

Mace had a small notebook of facts he'd pulled together before he'd even left Erie. He wasn't sure he liked a man who was so vain he'd name his town Hiho just to immortalize his name.

Of course, good ol' Hiram could have named it Humpsville.

That would be worse…much worse.

A small town in the middle of nowhere, celebrating its centennial.

When Mace dreamed about being a reporter, he dreamed about busting drug rings, exposing political corruption and reporting on mob activity. And here he was covering a small town's centennial, and doing a documentary on a man named Hiram Hump who wrote an obscure, yet acclaimed book of history. He was working at a station that didn't want hard-hitting stories. No, they wanted the nice news because it mattered.

Mace sighed. Maybe Stephanie was right. Maybe it was time to move on.

But first he had a story to report. It might not be a story he particularly wanted to tell, but Mace was professional enough to finish what he started.

He was supposed to meet his contact, Zoe Wallace, here in The General Store. The two-story building had a huge wooden porch, lined with rocking chairs. It was pretty much the center of Main Street.

Main Street. Not an overly creative name.

Neither was The General Store.

But Mace guessed if you lived in a community called Hiho, you probably wanted to keep everything else as simple as possible.

He glanced at his watch. Eleven-thirty. Right on time. He prided himself on being punctual and professional.

He got out of the car and went into the store. A bell rang as he pushed open the door.

It was like stepping back in time.

A huge fireplace. Checker boards, one with two older men playing a game. They didn't even look up as he came in.

More rocking chairs. And stuff. Lots and lots of stuff on shelves. Touristy looking stuff. Jars. Candles. Quilts.

A tall, blond woman stood behind a counter, an old-fashioned cash register between her and Mace. She smiled and asked, "Can I help you?"

"I'm supposed to meet Zoe Wallace here."

"Oh, you're just in time, which will annoy her. She was hoping you'd be late. Let me tell her you're here."

Why would this Zoe want him to be late?

The woman went to a door just beyond the counter and called, "Zoe, your appointment is out here. Best not keep him waiting."

A moment later, a woman emerged from a back room. He assumed it was Zoe Wallace and he suppressed a groan. It took every ounce of professionalism that Mace possessed to keep a straight face. She looked like…

Well, he didn't even have a frame of reference.

Her hair was big and he didn't need to be a hair stylist to know it was about twenty years out of style.

And her make-up…

Mace might know less about make-up than he did about hairstyles, but he knew that slashes of blue over eyelids were no longer considered eye shadow. And the garish shade of red on her lips would look right at home on any clown.

But worse than the make-up or hair, it appeared she'd tried to put on fake eyelashes, and one was drooping at the edge. He couldn't believe it wasn't making her crazy, tickling her eyeball as it wiggled with every blink of her eye.

Mace never noticed how much a person blinked, but either most people blinked a lot, or this Zoe was a compulsive blinker, but either way, the eyelash wiggled way too much.

"Um, Zoe Wallace?" he said, proud at how his voice never wavered.

She nodded, which caused the eyelash to jiggle even more.

Mace watched it, waiting for it to fall off completely, but her head stopped bobbling before it did.

"Theodore Mason?" Her voice was low and cultured. It didn't seem to fit with her outward appearance. "Do people call you Ted?"

"No…ah, they call me Mace."

"Mace Mason. It does have a ring. I'm just plain old Zoe." She thrust out a hand.

He didn't have the heart to tell her there was nothing plain about her. So, he simply took her hand in his and shook it. She had a warm, firm grip, but that eyelash wobbled as they shook. It was going to fall off. He was sure of it.

Forcing himself to ignore the eyelash, Mace said, "Nice to meet you, Zoe. I appreciate your taking the time to show me around the town."

He might be able to keep from laughing at her eyelash, but he wasn't sure he could keep the humor out of his voice when he said the town's name, so he planned to avoid saying the word *Hiho* at all costs.

"Your boss said you'd be spending most of the week tailing me, getting a feel for the town and some background on Hiram Hump."

She stared at him a moment, as if waiting for something, then suddenly she burst out laughing.

"Miss Wallace?" Mace said, not sure what she found so amusing.

"Call me Zoe," she gasped as she continued laughing. The woman behind the counter was laughing as well.

Darn. Did he have something stuck in this teeth? He ran his tongue over them, but didn't feel anything.

A hole in the seat of his pants?

No, Zoe was in front of him and wouldn't have seen it.

The women were both still laughing, one feeding off the other.

Oh, no. Was his fly unzipped?

Mace couldn't think of a circumspect way to check, so he glanced down.

Nope. The hatch was battened down.

"Is something wrong?" he finally asked.

Maybe the people in the town were as crazy as its name. That would be just like Steph to send him into the midst of an asylum.

"Oh, no," Zoe said, taking a deep breath and finally calming down. "I just have to say, you've impressed me in the first few seconds of meeting you, Mace. This should be an interesting week."

Impressed was better than amused, but still he didn't understand. "Impressed you how?"

"You didn't laugh."

She grinned at him, as if not laughing was some huge accomplishment. "You didn't crack a smile even. Clover—this is Clover Addison, by the way—and I had a bet at how long you could go without laughing, and I won. I said you were a professional and that you wouldn't laugh. And you didn't. Guess I'll have to spend my winnings buying you dinner."

"I still don't think I understand," Mace said.

"This," she said, waving at her hair and face. "You're the first person who's seen my *new look* and not laughed."

"You mean, this isn't your normal look?"

"Oh, I think I'm going to like you Mace Mason. I think I'm going to like you just fine. If you don't mind a quick trip to my house before we get started so I can un-make the make-over, I'd appreciate it."

"Sure," he said, not sure what else he could say.

"Come on." She held her hand out to Clover who slapped a ten-dollar bill into it.

"Come back in any time, Mace. It was a pleasure to meet a real gentleman." Clover shot a look at the men at the checkerboard and Mace assumed the comment was for their benefit.

"I might as well start your tour as we walk down Main Street," Zoe said. "I live two blocks from here."

She started down the street, still talking, and Mace followed.

Her makeover might be atrocious, but his view as he followed her was fine.

Mace gave his head a little shake. The last thing he needed was to be attracted to a small-town girl. He preferred his women a bit more sophisticated.

He caught up with Zoe, and walked right next to her.

She smiled at him and said, "Hiho, Ohio was founded by Hiram and Hortense Hump. The town's name came from the first two letters in their respective first names."

She must have seen him grimace, because she added, "Here in Hiho we say it could have been worse. It could have been—"

"Humpsville," he supplied.

She laughed again. "Right. Anyway, the town was incorporated in 1918. Our two biggest employers are Cloverleaf College and the Pawley Faucet Factory. We have—"

"Zoe," two voices cried in unison behind them.

She stopped and turned, and Mace followed suit. Two older women took one look at her and both cracked up.

"See what I mean," Zoe said. "That's been the normal response to my make-over, which is why you impressed me so much. Mace Mason, let me introduce Ida and Cora Macintosh. Two pillars of our community."

She turned back to the women. "Ladies, what can I do for you today?"

"Tom Walters," Ida said.

"What about Tom?" Zoe asked.

"You have him scheduled to judge the pie contest in the Festival," Cora said.

"And the problem is?" Zoe asked.

"He doesn't have any teeth. Cora and I are known for our apple pies, and they have walnuts in them. How on earth is Tom supposed to judge something like that fairly? He'll be predisposed to like the cream pies. And you know Betty is entering her chocolate, caramel pie. It's stiff competition in its own right, but with a toothless judge? We don't stand a chance."

"Ladies," Zoe said, in a voice designed to soothe. "I'll see to it that Tom wears his false teeth for the competition."

"But he hates them," Ida practically wailed.

"Regardless, if he wants to be a judge, he has to wear them."

"And if he won't?" Cora asked.

"Then I'll find a replacement."

"Fine. We trust you to see that the competition is fair, Zoe."

"I'll do my best, ladies. Now, if you don't mind, I think I need to turn back the hands of time and return to my usual self. Only don't tell Thelma Jean, okay?"

"Oh, we'd never hurt the old dear's feelings," Cora said.

"Thanks."

Mace grimaced as he listened to the ladies' emergency. A pie-judging scandal? He could just see the headlines now. *The Great Pie Dilemma.*

Nice news?

This didn't even qualify as drivel.

How on earth was he going to survive a whole week of this?

CHAPTER TWO

"This isn't what I expected," Mace murmured when he walked in her living room.

Zoe looked around the room, trying to decide just what he didn't expect about it. It wasn't as if there was anything that unusual about what the room contained. There was a couch, a couple of chairs, bookshelves, and a TV. Nothing special or out of the ordinary.

Okay, so the room was done completely in shades of white. White walls, furniture, and carpeting. Some people thought white was just one color, but there were shades and nuances. She wanted this room to emphasize that.

Everything was white except the arrangement of lilacs on the table. Deep and purple, they stood out in the room giving it a focus. Fresh flowers were her one indulgence.

"Are you surprised in a good way, or not?" she asked.

He shrugged. "Just surprised."

"What did you expect?"

He shrugged again. "Something more…well, more country-ish I guess."

"Ah, you expected Aunt Bee to be cooking in the kitchen baking cookies…she'd be wearing an apron, and would decorate with lots and lots of gingham, eh?"

Another shrug.

Zoe was ready to staple down his shoulders if he did it again. She wondered if he was shrugging as a gesture or maybe he had some kind of nervous tick.

She shrugged back at him, wondering if he'd notice she was mocking him.

He didn't seem to.

Men could be so dense. Even men who were reporters.

Since he didn't notice her mockery she settled for saying, "Sorry to disappoint."

She thought about trying to explain the effect she was going for, but decided against it. After all, she didn't care what Mace thought.

Instead she said, "Make yourself at home while I go change."

Aunt Bee indeed.

She walked through the dining room and into her bedroom, shutting her door with a little more force than it required.

She could have told Mace Mason that it wasn't all that long ago that she was living in a trendy section of Greenwich, working at a New York paper.

She could have told him about the people she'd met, the hard-hitting stories she broke…and the world-class ulcer she got.

She un-made her over-made makeover as quickly as possible. She pulled her big hair into a ponytail, pulled off the fake eyelashes and washed her face three times before she felt like herself again.

Feeling a hundred percent better, she went back out to her shoulder-shrugging guest.

He might be a big-city snob, but she was going to forgive his attitude because he hadn't laughed at her makeover.

He hadn't even cracked a smile.

So what if his surprise at her modern decor bordered on insulting? Maybe he didn't like modern decor and hadn't meant to be offensive at all. Maybe it had nothing to do with a big-city sense of superiority.

She pasted a smile on her well-washed face and went back into the living room. He was staring out the front bay window, a cell-phone at his ear. "…I can't stay the whole week. So far the biggest story I've got is the pie-judging scandal."

He paused.

"You heard me. Some old guy with dentures judging—" He stopped abruptly and said, "Listen, Stephanie, it doesn't matter. What does matter is you have to get me out of here. I'll stay the next couple days, get some footage then come home."

Another pause.

"I don't need to relax…Don't you tell me I'm terse. If I am it's only because you've sent me out in the middle of nowhere to cover the most non-news-worthy piece of drivel the world has ever known. WMAC has hit an all time low with this one…Don't tell me it's my job to make it news. Stephanie, don't you dare hang-up on me…"

He smacked the button on his cell phone so hard Zoe thought you might have damaged his finger.

She hoped it hurt. Because at the moment Zoe didn't care that Mace hadn't laughed at her appearance. She felt as if she was actually shimmering with anger.

So much for forgive and forget.

"Non-news-worthy, eh?" Zoe asked with a smile that threatened to break her jaw.

He whirled around. "You eavesdropped?"

"Not really." She let the smile drop because otherwise she was going to hurt herself. "You were just shouting so loud a herd of elephants could have walked through the room and you wouldn't have noticed."

He had the decency to look embarrassed. "Listen, it wasn't meant as a reflection on your town."

"Sure it was."

"It's just that this isn't what I imagined I'd be doing when I went into journalism."

Despite her annoyance, she felt a spurt of connection with this aggravating man. Once upon a time she'd had plans for her career and working in Hiho hadn't been one of them.

"Let me guess," she said softly. "You wanted bigger, better. Something with more pizzazz and more acclaim."

He didn't answer.

Didn't even shrug.

"Listen, Mace, we haven't known each other long, but let me assure you bigger isn't always better. Happy is."

He made a little scoffing noise. "With an attitude like that, you should be working at WMAC and not some little podunk paper."

"Pardon me?" The feeling of connection snapped. She was surprised he didn't hear the sound reverberate through the room.

"*WMAC, Where Nice News Matters.* Gag. You and *Pollyanna* Paige Montgomery would be best friends in no time. Want me to talk to my boss for you?"

"Listen, Mr. Mason, your first mild insult I put down to just…well, to your being a man. After you didn't laugh at my makeover, I figured I'd cut you some slack and overlook it. But this little town is my home and that *podunk paper* you're referring to is my livelihood. I am not going to cut you any slack if you're insulting either of them."

He raked a hand through his hair. "Listen, I'm sorry. I'm taking my annoyance out on you and that's not fair."

"You're right, it's not. And I'm sorry as well. Sorry that I thought…" She left the sentence hanging.

"What?" he pressed.

"I thought you were a nice guy. Instead, I see you're like so many other guys I've met in the business."

"How were those other guys."

She didn't answer, and he said, "Listen, I said, I'm sorry I insulted your paper and town."

"No, you're sorry *I heard you* insult my paper and town. There's a difference." She shook her head. It was like talking to a wall. "Never mind. We don't have to like or respect each other. I just have to show you around."

"You're still willing?" He sounded surprised.

"I told your editor I'd help you, and I will. I don't go back on my word just because someone is unpleasant, opinionated ... and wrong."

"Hey, don't hold anything back. Tell me how you see it." He offered her a small, non-condescending smile that said he knew he deserved whatever she dished out.

She couldn't help offering him a small one in return. "Hey, don't try and be funny now. You'll ruin my low opinion of you."

"Really, I am a nice guy. It's just that work isn't going the way I hoped and this trip just may be the final straw."

"I know," she said. "Bigger, better and all that."

She wished she could make him understand that if he got what he wanted he might find out he'd been wrong. Even as she thought it, she felt foolish. After all, maybe bigger and better was exactly what Mace Mason wanted. She'd known him for all of—what an hour? His dreams were his own and absolutely none of her business.

"So why don't I apologize again for putting my foot in my mouth." He shot her another one of those grins that the camera probably ate up. "I really am sorry and would like to start over, if that's okay with you."

"Apology accepted. I don't like seeing reporters make sweeping generalizations. You can't report accurately if you come into a story with a bias. And you, Mr. Mason, are biased against small towns."

He paused a moment, as if considering her words, then finally said, "So convince me I'm wrong."

"I will."

Zoe Wallace was a babe.

That much was apparent as soon as she unmade that makeover.

Black shoulder-length hair and her eyes…well, they were blue, but that just didn't seem like an accurate description. Mace could think of a bunch of adjectives that would clarify the color—robin's egg blue, sky blue, jewel blue—but he wasn't about to use any of them. They sounded far too…just *too*.

No, black hair, blue eyes. That was as far as he planned to go with a description.

But he would allow that she was drop-dead gorgeous. Not only that, but she could hold her own in a fight. That might not seem like something that would impress him, but it was. Mace had dated too many women who couldn't, or wouldn't, take him on. Mace enjoyed a good verbal sparring now and again.

Zoe had been right to call him on the carpet for his unthinking remarks.

Oh, she was still mad, but he had hopes he could tease her out of her funk. He'd already gotten one smile, maybe he could get more?

Why he cared if she was mad at him, he wasn't sure, but he did.

Her gait was brisk and rippling with her annoyance. Time to try the old *Mason* charm.

"Hey, it's not a marathon," he finally said, in what he hoped was a teasing, endearing tone.

"It's late and it's been a long day," she snapped back.

"Yeah, but—"

She interrupted him with a sigh. "So, let's grab a quick bite, like I promised, and get you settled so we can make an early start of it tomorrow."

She stopped abruptly a few doors down from The General Store. "Here we go."

Obviously his tone hadn't been endearing enough because she was still annoyed.

He didn't know her well enough to tease her out of her snit, so he simply followed her to the diner. It was built in to a long stretch of brick establishments. The window proudly proclaimed it, *Pete's Eats.*

"You're kidding, right?" he asked.

She whirled around, ready to fight, and Mace wished he'd kept his mouth shut about the establishment's name. "What?"

"Nothing," he said, hoping to stave off another battle.

Zoe sighed. "The owner's name is Pete, and … well, it's a great place to eat. Honesty in advertising, I'd say."

"But—" he started.

She interrupted him again. "Listen, when you live in a town called Hiho—"

"You keep things simple." He grinned. "I'd already reached that conclusion."

Some of Zoe's icy demeanor melted enough to allow her to offer him another small smile in return. "You've got it. And you'll love the food here. Pete's wife Alice does most of the cooking, and I dare say there's nothing in a bigger city to rival it. Before the week is out you'll feel like a regular. Just wait and see."

She pushed open the door and led him into a small dining room. Red and white checked table clothes, bright sunny yellow walls.

Mace took it all in and then stopped himself. Since when did he notice decor?

First at The General Store he'd noted the rustic-nostalgic look, then at Zoe's place he'd been taken aback by her decorating style. All that white had him thinking of ice—an ice princess just waiting for someone to thaw her out. When she emerged un-made-over, Mace had actually thought he might enjoy trying to warm her up.

The thought had scared him—not the warming Zoe up part, but the noticing how places were decorated part. After all, what man noticed something like that?

Yet here he was looking at the interior of *Pete's Eats* and he'd actually thought the words *sunny yellow*.

He was thankful he didn't say them out loud. And he was even happier that he was only staying through Sunday because the town was already messing with his mind. Pretty soon he'd be using words like *ambiance* and *accent*.

If he did and Steph overheard, no one would be able to save him. She'd have him doing an in-depth report on interior design. There was a relatively new designer in Erie who ran *By Designs* that everyone was raving about. Steph would make him report on that.

Talk about a non-news story.

"Do you prefer a table or booth?" Zoe asked.

Mace realized he'd been lost in decorating thoughts, which was preferable to thinking about Zoe as an ice princess in need of waking.

"Doesn't matter," he said.

She led him to a corner booth and moments after they were seated, a small man approached the table. "Zoe, honey, how are you?"

"Just fine, Pete. How's Alice?" she asked.

"Fit as a fiddle. She saw you come in and says to tell you she's got your favorite back there."

"Then I don't even have to think about what I'm ordering." She shut the menu and looked at Mace.

"Ah, just what is your favorite?" Mace asked as he glanced at the menu, which was conveniently printed on the place mat.

"You won't find it on the menu," Zoe said. "It doesn't need to be advertised. Trust me, you'll like it."

"Fine. I'll have what she's having," he told Pete, who hurried back toward the kitchen.

"Daring, eh? Well, there may be some hope for you yet, Mace Mason," Zoe said, offering him a smile...a real smile.

"Seriously, I'm sorry you overheard me. It's really not the town. It's frustration. My boss sent me for the week to relax."

"You don't look very relaxed to me," she pointed out.

"You're observant nature must be what led you to reporting," he said, knowing that his tone had come out less than friendly—some might even call it terse.

Zoe tapped her fingers on the tabletop as she frowned.

"Sorry," he mumbled.

What was it about this woman that had him behaving like a buffoon?

"Listen," she said, her fingers still beating a fast rhythm. "I don't want to spend my week sparring with you. I have too much to do as it is. Let's just forget that I overheard you and that I now know you're not happy about being in Hiho. We'll start all over again."

She held her hand out across the table. "Hi. You must be Mace Mason. I'm Zoe Wallace of the Hiho Herald."

"Nice to meet you, Zoe. You can't imagine how nice." Mace shook her hand and desperately tried not to notice how warm it felt in his. More than warm, it felt...

He dropped her hand as quickly as he dropped the thought. He didn't come here for a fling with some *podunk* reporter.

Podunk. He felt better having thought the word. Not that he was ever going to say it out loud again, but he'd think it all he wanted.

Podunk.

Podunk.

Podunk.

Unfortunately this particular *podunk* reporter looked just as good after he thought the words as before.

"So, where would you like to start?" she asked. Before he could answer, she added, "The real Centennial festivities don't pick up until this weekend. By the way, you're invited to a dinner Friday night at the college. It will be a great opportunity to introduce you around."

"Thanks."

"But that leaves you a lot of time. You're welcome to follow me as I take care of the final arrangements, but that's not exactly news."

"*Not exactly news.* That's exactly the kind of stuff WMAC covers." He sighed then, a sigh that spoke of frustration with work. "But you're right, I don't want to spend the next few days dogging your every step. Maybe some of them, but not all of them. What I'd hoped is that you could hook me up with some of the town's archives. I don't know if Stephanie explained exactly what I do."

"She just said you were doing an in-depth piece."

"I am. I'll be shooting footage of the Festival, but in addition I'm gathering background information about Hiram Hump for *Erie Chronicles*. Chronicles are half hour segments about Erie's history. We tie our subjects to current events, things we can use on the news, and then run the specials. It allows us to cross-promote."

Pete came over and put a mug of coffee in front of each of them.

"Thanks, Pete," Zoe said.

Pete gave a noncommittal grunt and walked back toward the kitchen.

"But why cover Hiram Hump?" she asked.

"You do know he was from Erie, right?" Mace noted that Zoe loaded her coffee up with cream and sugar. He realized he was paying attention to all sorts of small things about her. Not just how she took her coffee, but also the way she tapped her fingers against the table when he annoyed her.

That he noticed anything about her was disconcerting. He tried to tell himself that it was the reporter in him, but it sounded hollow even to him.

"Of course I know Hiram's from Erie. We value our history here, which is why this Centennial is such a big deal."

"Well, he wrote some obscure, but valued history and my editor thought—"

A voice interrupted him. "*Psst*, Zoe."

She turned. "Bertram, I—"

"Don't turn around," the voice barked. "Don't let them know I'm talking to you."

She obeyed and swung back around to face Mace, who could see the back of the head of the man who was *pssting* Zoe.

"So, have you found out anything?" the *psster* asked.

"Not yet, Bertram, but I'm planning on checking. I promise."

The *psster* turned around and Mace got a glimpse of a life-lined man with thin grey hair. A man—Bertram Zoe had called him—who was studying him, suspicion in his narrowed eyes.

"Who's he? A spy for them?" Bertram asked.

"No. He's a... a friend."

"Okay." He gave Mace a quick nod, then turned back around and continued, "This is the biggest story Hiho has ever had. I tried to talk to Pawley about the endowments, but even he doesn't want to hear. Said he couldn't do anything without proof. We need to get that proof and they don't want us to get it. So be careful. They're watching me all the time. I managed to sneak away, but it's only a matter of time until Pete spots me here and—"

"Uncle Bertram," Pete said right on cue. He swooped in like some angry hornet and set plates filled with meatloaf and mashed potatoes on their table with a decisive slam as he continued talking to the *psster*. "You know you're supposed to be in the back helping Alice today."

"Just taking a break, Pete. Resting my tired old feet," Bertram said in a voice that did indeed sound tired.

"*Old* isn't the word I'd use to describe you," Pete said with an inflection that made Mace wonder just what word the waiter would use to describe his uncle.

Pete continued, "Come on, let's go into the kitchen before Alice comes out."

Mace thought he might like to meet this Alice who struck so much fear into grown men.

Or maybe he wouldn't.

"Hope he wasn't bothering you, Zoe," Pete said.

"Of course not," Zoe said. "Why I didn't even know he was back there until you said something."

Pete looked as if he didn't quite believe her, but finally nodded and said, "Well, that's good. Enjoy your dinner. Come on, Uncle."

"Don't forget what I said, Zoe," Bertram whispered as he obligingly followed Pete into the kitchen.

"What was that all about?" Mace asked, not sure what to make of the cloak-and-dagger foolery.

"Nothing. Bertram is a bit...eccentric."

"Oh," he replied noncommittally, but he sensed Zoe wasn't being entirely truthful with him. He'd been a reporter for too long to miss that something was up.

Granted, what he'd been doing lately wasn't very good reporting, but that didn't mean he wasn't a very good reporter.

He sensed a story.

"Try your meatloaf," Zoe said.

Mace speared the meat, regretting he'd followed her lead. He wasn't overly enthusiastic about meatloaf as a rule.

"About that man—" he started.

But she interrupted. "Come on, try it."

He took a small bite and knew at that moment that no matter how scary Alice was, if her meatloaf could taste this good, he could learn to like her.

"This is..." he let the sentence trail off, not how sure how to describe what he was eating.

"Yeah, it's that good. I think it's the mozzarella cheese that does it."

He grunted his agreement.

"About your schedule," she said.

Mace couldn't have proved it in a court of law, but he sensed Zoe was anxious to talk about anything except her *psster*.

"I'll get you settled for the night," she continued, just a little to hurriedly, "and we can get you started first thing in the morning. I'll take you over to the college and introduce you around. In addition to the campus library itself, they have an exhibit on Hiram that I think would be helpful to you. You can dig around for information there."

"That would be great. And the paper? Can I possibly have access to your archives as well?"

Zoe didn't look exceptionally pleased with the request, but she finally nodded. "Sure."

She dug through her purse and handed him a key. "You can use this for the duration of your stay. It's for the back door. Help yourself."

"Great." He took the key and pocketed it. "Thanks. So, how far is my hotel?"

She hesitated. "Ah, did your boss tell you that you were staying at a hotel?"

"She just said you'd get me settled."

"And I will, but you see, Hiho has one hotel and it's booked solid for the whole week. There's one back on the interstate about fifteen miles from here, but I thought you'd prefer to stay in Hiho."

"So if not the hotel, where am I staying? Please tell me not with you."

The minute the words were out of his mouth he realized they could be interpreted as terse, and wished he could suck them back in.

But Zoe didn't seem to take offense this time. In fact, she laughed. "Don't worry. You're not staying with me. Your boss had me book you a room at Aunt Aggie's Bed and Breakfast. I think you'll like it there. In addition to making the best muffins in the world, Aunt Aggie has that *Aunt Bee* quality you seemed to expect to find in the women of Hiho ..."

CHAPTER THREE

Zoe was right, Aunt Aggie made the best muffins Mace had ever tasted. It would have been the perfect place to stay if it wasn't for her evil looking pit bull, Baby.

He was pretty sure that Baby didn't like him.

And he was more than sure that he wasn't fond of Baby.

But Baby wasn't the reason he was feeling quite out-of-sorts this morning.

Oh, his room was comfortable—even his bed was—but he couldn't sleep.

All because of Zoe Wallace.

Every time he closed his eyes he dreamt of her.

Laughing.

Sputtering.

Fighting mad.

He couldn't seem to shake thoughts of her.

And now walking next to her on the way to Cloverleaf College he wondered if Zoe had a car, because she seemed to walk everywhere and it wasn't improving his mood.

She kept a running monologue of the town's history. "…that Clover was a women's libber and intended to make the college women's only. But then she met Lief Johnson and he convinced her to marry him and taught her men had their uses, so it was a co-ed college. The Clover you met at the General Store is their descendent…"

Mace was finding it hard to focus on what Zoe was saying because his attention was on her face.

It was an average face, as far as he could tell. A basic looking nose. Two eyes. A mouth that hadn't stopped moving. Everything where it should be. Fairly nice symmetry. Nothing extraordinary.

And yet, even without a fake eyelash bobbling against her eye, he couldn't seem to stop watching her.

"...We had the Centennial Beauty Pageant last week. Katy Sloane, the town librarian won, but abdicated her crown to Brandi Rankin. You'll meet Brandi at the dinner later this week. But watch out for her mom ... when she finds out you're an out-of-town reporter you're going to have a hard time shaking her. Brandi will kick off the Festival by leading the parade on Saturday morning. We'll wrap things up Sunday night with a huge firework display. The Centennial Celebration has been such an economic boon for the community—"

Her sentence stopped dead in its tracks and so did she.

Zoe was staring at something. Before Mace could turn and see what, she sprinted across the grassy park.

What was she doing now?

He'd known her less than twenty-four hours, but already suspected that she wasn't a normal sort of woman.

Bad makeovers. Cloak and dagger meetings.

Running across the park after a ...

A bull?

Not just any bull.

A big bull.

Giant even.

Man, if you painted the thing blue it could have belonged to Paul Bunyan himself.

"Zoe," he cried, squeezing her name past the huge lump in his throat.

"Zoe!"

He sprinted after her, although he didn't have a clue what he could do to prevent the giant bull from attacking her and trampling her to the ground.

He didn't know anything about cattle and suddenly wished he did. What good was knowing about English literature or even journalism in a situation like this?

"Zoe, damn it, stop!"

His warning was too late. She had something in her hand.

It was her belt, he realized.

She'd taken off her belt and was going to lasso it around the bull's thick neck. It would kill her.

"Hey! Hey bull," Mace called.

The stupid thing was probably going to gore him, but at least Zoe would get away.

"Bull!" he screamed, trying to get it to come toward him rather than Zoe.

He waved his hand, wishing he had something red. That was the color bulls liked he was pretty sure.

"Bull!"

Visions of Zoe gored by the beast flashed through his head.

"Bull!"

The bull turned and just stared at him with a rather bored expression on its big, homely face.

If someone had asked him yesterday he would have denied that a bull could look bored, but this one did.

Zoe slipped the belt over its neck, then patted it and murmured something in its ear.

Mace approached more slowly, not wanting to spook the giant beast now that Zoe was holding on.

"What are you doing?" he asked trying to keep his voice soft and calm.

Other than being slightly out of breath, she looked none the worse for wear. As a matter of fact, she shot him a dazzling sort of smile. "You tried to save me. That's why you were shouting, right? To get the bull to chase you instead of going after me?"

Mace shrugged, unsure what to say. Zoe didn't look overly moved by his shot at heroics. To be honest, she looked slightly amused.

"Sorry if I scared you. There was nothing to worry about. Jed here is one step from the grave and doesn't have the stamina to chase after you. Where he gets the energy to walk to the campus every day is a bit of a mystery. If he was any other bull, Don David would have gotten rid of him long ago. But he holds onto him because he's sentimental. Don's sentimental, not the bull. Although, Jed may be as well."

"Well, this Don David should keep the beast locked up."

"Nothing Don does can keep Jed penned. No fence is high enough or strong enough." She covered the bull's ears. "You see, Jed has a crush on Bessie, the college's mascot. He likes to visit."

"Pardon?"

"The college's mascot is a bison—The Cloverleaf Bisons. They don't have enough money to buy one yet—though we do have a Buffalo fund—so Don donated Bessie to sort of fill in until they raise enough for a real bison. And Jed misses her. Love's like that. Sometimes there's just nothing you can do to stop it. It will break through any obstacle."

"Oh, no," Mace groaned.

"What?" Zoe asked.

"Not only are you crazy enough to chase after a bull—"

"He's gentle as a lamb," Zoe argued.

Mace ignored her and kept right on talking, "But you're also a romantic."

"So?"

"Honey—"

"Don't call me honey." Her terminal good cheer evaporated just like that.

"*Zoe*," Mace said with emphasis. "Love is just an excuse to propagate."

A man came running up to them. His face lit up when he saw Zoe and the bull. "You got him."

"Yes. You know, you've really got to watch him this week, Don. It's going to be crazy what with the festival going on. I know Jed's sweet, but I'd hate to see him get scared by the crowd."

"I'm taking him out to Old Mac's farm. Figure even if he gets out, we could catch him long before he gets all the way into town. Mac's a lot further out than I am. I was just getting ready to load him into the truck when he got away. Thanks for catching him."

"Glad to help."

He slipped a rope around the bull's neck and handed Zoe her belt before leading Jed, the lovelorn bull, down the street.

"Old Mac?" Mace asked.

Zoe threaded her belt through the loops on her pants and a small sliver of her stomach showed. Just a tiny little band of skin. Nothing overt, not even overly sexy. And yet, Mace couldn't tear his eyes away.

She finished, tucked her shirt back in place—much to his disappointment—and looked at him and grinned. "Mac's last name is MacDonald and he—"

"Has a farm?" Mace supplied.

"Yep."

"This whole town is insane," Mace muttered. He felt rather proud that he didn't add,_and you're the biggest lunatic in this asylum.

"Maybe... but we're happy. Can you say as much, Mace?"

"I don't know where you got the idea I'm not happy," Mace said, not caring if he sounded annoyed.

First Stephanie said he was terse and needed to take a vacation, and now Zoe—an utter stranger—was telling him he was unhappy.

Like he should listen to what a crazy woman who lassoed bulls with her belt said.

"I'm deliriously happy at this moment in time... happy you didn't get yourself killed by that beast."

"Like I said, Jed wouldn't hurt a fly. He's sort of a town fixture. And Mace, I know happy when I see it, and you're not happy... delirious or otherwise."

"I am happy," he insisted.

"Nope, you're not." She smiled then. It was the same smile that had punctuated his dreams last night. Hot dreams. A smile that begged him to do just what he'd done in those dreams.

And before he could think about it and talk himself out of it, Mace did just what he'd done in his dreams.

He kissed her.

Only on the cheek. Just a reaction to her battle with the bull he was sure.

It didn't mean anything.

It was practically platonic.

Of course, *practically* was the key word.

Because he wasn't feeling totally platonic about Zoe Wallace.

Not at all.

And that didn't make sense because she wasn't the kind of woman he was attracted to. He wanted someone sophisticated, someone career oriented with goals and ambitions that went beyond some podunk paper, someone …

Yet, he looked at her, standing there, looking dazed, staring at him, and knew that though it didn't make sense, though he barely knew her, he wanted her. Not in a physical way, but more than that. He wanted to argue with her and laugh with her. He wanted her to smile at him.

"Zoe?" he finally said.

She gave herself a little shake, as if she was coming out of a trance. "Why on earth did you do that?"

"I was just relieved your weren't gored to death. It was a platonic thing. Heck, Europeans do that cheek kiss stuff all the time."

"We're not European."

"Yeah, I don't think anyone would think Hiho, Ohio was a cosmopolitan European city."

"Well …" She paused a moment, then said, "Well, don't do it again."

"Okay. But only if you promise not to chase after any more bulls."

"Deal." She held out her hand, as if to shake on it, then dropped it immediately.

Mace was glad because he really wanted to touch her … which meant he'd have to avoid touching her at all costs.

"Let's go and get you situated at the college," she said as she started walking toward the college again. "I have stuff to do."

"Fine."

❧ ❧ ❧

MEN!

Zoe thought the word in all caps and with an exclamation point.

MEN!

That one word kept interrupting the thousand things she had to do for the Festival.

Zoe might be able to handle the paper and the Centennial details, juggling them all and so far without dropping any. But she didn't know how to handle Mace Mason. She couldn't keep up with him.

First he was nice and didn't laugh at her crazy makeover, then he was a heel, referring to her paper as podunk.

She wasn't sure precisely what *podunk* was, but she was pretty sure it wasn't a compliment.

Then he'd tried to save her from Jed, trying to get the bull to chase him rather than her. Not that Jed would chase anyone, but Mace hadn't known that. He thought he was risking his life with a giant bull to save her. That made him a hero.

All the waffling to and from nice guy status, she could deal with and almost understand. After all, men were fickle creatures and no sane woman could truly understand how their minds worked.

But then Mace had kissed her.

He was right. She'd kissed babies and elderly friends on the cheeks on occasion. It wasn't sexual.

But for a moment, it felt like there was something more than Mace's relief in it.

And for an even briefer moment, Zoe was pleased about that.

She couldn't begin to understand it.

She couldn't decide if it made him nicer or a bigger heel. So she forced herself to concentrate on the copy she was supposed to be proofing.

Someone cleared their throat and she just about jumped out of her seat.

"Earth calling Zoe," Clover said with a smile.

"Sorry. Just lost in thought. I didn't even hear you come in. Did you need something, or is this just social?"

"Maybe a little of both." She paused and looked around the small office. "Where's your hunky reporter?"

"He's not mine and he's not that hunky."

Zoe crossed her fingers beneath the counter. That was a lie—not the part about him not being hers … he wasn't. But the other part, the hunky part, well he was gorgeous but she wasn't going to admit it to Clover.

"You haven't noticed the way his eyes are so brown they're almost black?"

"No. Brown is brown. And I think I read somewhere that it's the most common eye color, so his eyes can't be all that special if more people share their color than any other."

"I don't think anyone has quite the same color eyes that he does. At least not here in Hiho. I don't know if you noticed it, but there's a certain dearth in eligible men here."

"No, I hadn't noticed," Zoe said, though that was a lie as well.

"Come on, even Vic noticed, and she hardly ever knows what day of the week it is."

"Sure she does, she's the mayor after all. She's got a fine mind for details." Knowing Vicky, she'd probably not only noticed the shortage of eligible men, but had some new plan up her sleeves to get some more bachelors to move to town. Vicky was a driving force in the town's recent growth.

Rather than look for new industry, she was encouraging people to look for ways to attract tourism to the area.

"Vic's got an eye for the job, but not much else. But it's that lack of eligible men that made me think about asking Mace out. But I won't if you're interested in him."

"Interested in Mace Mason?" Zoe laughed at the thought. Although the laughter sounded a bit odd to her ears. Clover didn't seem to notice. In fact she smiled, so Zoe continued, "What kind of name is Mace anyway?"

"A nice one?" Clover said.

"Pretentious, that's what it is. Mace Mason." She thought it was cute when she first met him, but since he'd kissed her she'd decided it was best not to think of Mace as cute in any way. "But that's not what you asked. To answer your question, no I'm not interested in him. After all, he's only here for the week."

"A lot can happen in a week." The gleam in Clover's eyes gave Zoe an indication about just how much Clover would like to happen.

"I don't think a personality change can happen that quick."

"What do you mean?" Clover asked.

"He doesn't like our little *podunk* town." She could feel herself bristle all over again as she remembered the conversation. Bristling over the conversation was better than melting over his kiss. "He feels that covering podunk little Hiho's Centennial is beneath him."

"Well maybe I can change his mind."

"I doubt it." Short of having a brain transplant, Zoe didn't see any hopes for Mace's mind changing.

"But you don't mind if I try?" Clover asked.

"I already said I didn't," Zoe said. Even as the words came out of her mouth, she realized they'd sounded a bit abrupt, so she added a, "Really," in hopes of softening them.

Clover studied her a moment. Zoe tried to resist the urge to squirm under her scrutiny.

"Really," she said again.

"You say you don't mind, but I'm not sure that's what you mean."

"I'm a reporter. I always say exactly what I mean."

Why would she care if Mace had dinner with Clover?

To be honest, she was more nervous that Clover was having dinner with Mace. Clover was so sweet, Mace could really hurt her. "Just be careful."

Clover laughed. "I think I can handle Mace Mason. And if you're sure you don't mind—"

Zoe interrupted. "I'm sure."

"—I'm going to ask him to dinner tonight, all right?"

"Sure. He planned on spending the day at the college digging around, then he was going to meet me back here at the office at four."

"So, I'll go catch him at the college, and if he's interested we can do dinner when you're done with him."

Done with him?

Zoe had been done with Mace Mason the moment he kissed her.

She was past done with him. She was…she couldn't think of an appropriate phrase, but she was way past being done with him.

"No problem. Just be careful," she warned Clover again.

"Why?"

"I wouldn't want you to expect more from Mace than he can give."

Clover looked at her for an inordinately long time. "Are you sure about this?"

"Sure I'm sure." Geesh, how many times did she have to say it? "I have absolutely no designs on Mace."

After all, one quick bull-induced kiss on the cheek didn't mean anything at all. Why Mace probably kissed hundreds of women.

The fact her knees had practically buckled had more to do with the fact she'd sprinted after Jed, not the fact Mace kissed her. Okay, so maybe a little because Mace kissed her, but that was probably due to her rather lengthy date-less existence than anything to really to do with Mace's kissing ability.

"Positive," she added when Clover still stood waiting.

"Well, okay. I'm going to go find him now."

"Good luck. See you later."

This was great. If Mace was occupied with Clover tonight, Zoe should have time to go dig around the paper's archives and see if she could find any proof to Bertram's wild statements.

And if she found the proof, what would she do?

It would certainly be a big story, and as a journalist she'd be obligated to print it.

But the college had already borrowed against that endowment. If they had to wait another year for it to come through…well, Zoe didn't know what that would mean to them financially, but it couldn't be good.

Of course the library was counting on the money for renovations and improvements. Why, Katy Sloane had practically glowed last time they talked, as she speculated at all she could do with that money.

Zoe shook her head.

Maybe before she went digging she should talk to Rob Pawley, who was overseeing the endowments for the college and the library, and see just what sort of implications Bertram's accusations could have on the entire community.

One more thing on her list of things to do.

Why it was great that Clover was taking Mace out tonight because truly, she didn't have time to play nursemaid for him.

Yes, Zoe was thrilled that Clover was taking Mace off her hands.

Mace walked the four blocks between the college and the newspaper with long, brisk steps.

Some people might think they were angry steps, but of course they weren't. After all, what did he have to be angry about?

Zoe practically threw him at another woman, but Clover, the woman in question, was gorgeous and ran her own successful business, which indicated she had a brain.

Beautiful and intelligent. A winning combination.

So Mace should be grateful for the fix-up.

But he wasn't.

He was annoyed.

After all, he'd kissed Zoe—albeit just on the cheek—in the afternoon and, before he'd gotten himself back under control, she was throwing him at another woman.

It wasn't very flattering.

As a matter of fact, it was almost insulting.

Oh, Mace didn't suffer under any delusions that he was a lady's man. But he also knew that he wasn't some boy-toy to get shared between friends.

Yes, Clover seemed nice enough and he'd said yes to her dinner invitation, but…

He wasn't sure just what his *but* was, but he knew that he was annoyed with Zoe, which he guessed that was pretty fair since she seemed to spend a great deal of time annoyed with him.

He walked into Pete's Eats and couldn't even work up a good snicker for the restaurant's name. That was just another small indication of how deeply annoyed he was.

He looked around and didn't see Clover.

He glanced at his watch. He was early. He found it difficult to gauge how long it took to walk somewhere. Erie was a driving town. But here in Hiho, everyone seemed to walk everywhere.

He slid into a booth towards the back and settled in to wait.

Pete came over. "Waiting for Zoe?"

"No. For Clover Addison."

Pete studied him a moment and then said, "Well, can I get you something while you wait. And I should tell you that you may wait a while so you probably should order something."

He glanced at his watch again. "I'm not that early."

"No, but Clover tends to live in a different time zone than the rest of us. As a matter of fact, I don't recall her ever arriving anywhere on time. Why, her mother used to say when Clover was two weeks late being born it was just an indication of how the girl's life would be lived."

"Oh."

"Most of the town tells her to be somewhere at least a half hour before they need her there simply because she's always late. I don't suppose you thought to do that."

"Why would I?" he asked.

"Well, yes, there's that. Well, you just sit back and relax. What would you like to drink while you wait?"

"Coffee."

Pete looked concerned. "Don't you think it's a little late for coffee? I mean, its bound to keep you up. And if you don't mind my saying, you look like you could use a good sleep."

Mace wasn't going to ask just what Pete meant by that. He didn't want to know if the fact he'd spent last night thinking about Zoe was that evident, that he looked that tired.

"Coffee," he repeated and immediately realized how short he'd sounded.

Pete must have realized it as well, because he didn't argue further. "Far be it from me to interfere. Coffee it is."

He hustled away before Mace could apologize, then hurried back with the coffee, set it down with a distinct clunk, and left again.

Great. Mace was systematically alienating the town. First Zoe handed him off like a hot potato, and now Pete was annoyed with him as well.

Mace sipped his coffee and stewed over…well over everything. His life was out of control and he wasn't sure how to reclaim it.

He thought about Zoe's makeover and realized maybe it was time for him to makeover his life. Maybe he should put out feelers for a new job.

He sighed and took a sip of coffee.

Zoe's little, *bigger isn't better, happy is,* phrase kept running through his mind.

He was happy dammit.

Almost on cue, she entered the restaurant. She gave a little wave to a man and headed over to his table, her back to Mace.

All thoughts of happy fled as he watched her sit down with the guy.

Who was that?

The man was blond, and even from this distance, Mace could tell he had a weak chin. He didn't look like he could stand up to a Chihuahua, much less Zoe.

What was she doing with a guy like that? She'd eat him alive.

Not that Mace cared.

"Hi, is this seat taken?" a voice asked, startling Mace.

A very female voice.

He looked up and Clover Addison stood next to the booth smiling at him.

"Oh, you're early."

She glanced at her watch. "Actually, I'm running a little late."

"But not as late as I was told to expect."

He heard the words come out of his mouth and wanted to kick himself. What was happening to him? Terse was one thing, but rude was another.

Clover didn't seem to mind. She smiled as she sat down. "I see you were forewarned. I always mean to be on time, but life always seems to get in the way."

She waved at Pete and called, "Just an ice water with lemon," then turned back to Mace.

"You see, I was all ready to close the store and be here on time when..."

He glanced at Zoe. What was that? She passed some papers, or maybe a file, across the table to the man.

"...and the man said, 'But I need chains...'"

The blond guy was looking at the folder—it had been a folder—and slammed it back to the table, a scowl on his face.

It wasn't much of a scowl because it was hard to manage a good one with such a weak chin.

Mace didn't think he was conceited, but he knew he could out-scowl that guy any day of the week.

Out-chin him as well.

"...but his wife said that vacation or not, she just wasn't into that kind of thing..."

Zoe and the mystery man were exchanging heated words. Mace strained, trying to hear what they were saying, but they were obviously disagreeing, their voices were hushed and he couldn't make out a thing.

"…So what do you think?" Clover asked.

"Think?" Mace asked, tearing his gaze away from Zoe and concentrating on the woman sitting across from him.

What had she been talking about? A man who wanted chains and a wife who wasn't inclined to play those kinds of games even on vacation.

"Yes, what do you think?" Clover repeated. "Do you think I should expand my merchandise selection to include something like that? I mean, I know you're not in retail, but you're from a bigger city and I'd value your opinion."

"I'll confess I'm not into kinky things," he said, glancing over Clover's shoulder to where Zoe and Mr. Weak-chin were still going at it.

"Kinky?" Clover asked. "You think antique light fixtures are kinky?"

"You weren't talking light fixtures, you were talking about chains," he said.

"To hang wagon wheel chandeliers from the ceiling," Clover said slowly, as if he were just a little slow.

"Oh."

"Chains," she murmured and chuckled. "Yes, that would be a big change in my merchandise."

The laughter faded and she smiled at him as she said, "Mace, if you'd rather not do this, I understand."

"No, really, it's not that. It's just that…Who's that man with Zoe?" He pointed to the booth on the opposite side of the restaurant.

Clover turned around and looked. "Rob. Robert Pawley. He's a lawyer. His family's as much an institution in Hiho as mine."

"How is that?" Mace asked.

"His family came into town about the same time the first member of my family did. The Pawley's started The Pawley Faucet Factory, though they gave up controlling interest a long time ago. Rob still manages the family trust."

"And he's seeing Zoe?" Mace asked and then wished he hadn't. He didn't want Clover to think he cared who Zoe dated. No, he simply wondered what was going on between them.

"No. Actually, he was dating Katy Sloane until last week."

"Katy Sloane?" He thought he'd heard the name, but with the way Zoe babbled great quantities of town information at him, he wasn't sure who she was.

"The town librarian. She won the beauty pageant, but abdicated to Brandi Rankin."

Aha! That's where he'd heard the name.

Zoe continued, "Katy's story is a fun one. You see—"

Mace interrupted her. "So if this Pawley and Zoe aren't seeing each other, what are they talking about. Almost fighting about, by the looks of things."

Clover turned around again and studied the pair a moment, then turned back and faced Mace. "I don't have a clue. Rob is in charge of the big endowment for the college and the library. He'll be presenting the checks at the Festival's closing ceremonies. Maybe that's what they're talking about. It makes sense, since Zoe's in charge of the Festival."

"But they're not talking, they're fighting," he said.

Oh, it wasn't much of a fight. He didn't imagine a weak-chinned guy like Pawley knew much about the finer art of fighting.

Now when he fought with Zoe … that was fighting. He liked that she could stand toe-to-toe with him and not flinch. He liked that she could call him on things when he deserved it.

"Like I said, I can't imagine why they'd be fighting," Clover said.

"So, what will you have tonight?" Pete asked.

He shot a nasty look at Mace.

Yep, he should have listened to the waiter and skipped the coffee. Maybe if he left a big tip Pete would get over it.

"I'd like spaghetti," Clover said. "Ranch dressing on the salad."

"And you?" Pete asked Mace.

"Whatever she's having," Mace said not caring what he ate. He was far too interested in the situation at Zoe's booth.

"Mace, this was a mistake, wasn't it?" Clover asked softly when Pete left.

He forced himself to concentrate on his date. "What was a mistake?"

"I'd hoped that we could get to know each other while you were visiting, but that's not going to happen, is it?"

"Sure. I'd planned on coming over to talk to you about the first Clover here in Hiho who founded the college. I need background for my Chronicle piece, and she seems to have had an important role in the town. After all, the college and the faucet factory are the biggest employers in the area and …"

He glanced from Clover to Zoe's table and his sentence trailed off.

That Pawley guy was getting up and stalking towards the door.

Stalking.

As if he was annoyed.

More than annoyed—mad.

Of course, with that weak chin he couldn't carry off anger any better than he could carry off a scowl, but he seemed to be doing his best impersonation of anger.

"I rest my case," Clover said.

Zoe was just sitting there at the table, all alone. Her back was facing him, so he couldn't tell if she was upset.

He'd go find that weak-chinned Pawley guy if he made Zoe cry.

Not that he cared about Zoe. At least not in any man-woman sort of way.

Of course there was that kiss.

But that was just the heat of the moment, European sort of kiss.

After all, she'd almost been killed by a killer bull. Of course he kissed her, just to make sure she was still alive.

"Earth calling Mace," Clover said.

"Sorry. Just wondering what was up with that guy and Zoe. He left and she's there all alone. Maybe she's crying. Maybe they were dating and you didn't know it. Maybe he broke it off, breaking her heart."

"He was dating Katy last week and, to be honest, Rob is sort of bland. I don't think he has it in him to be dating anyone else that fast, much less break her heart. Plus, this is a small town. If they were dating, then I'd have heard. Like I said, it was probably Centennial business."

"I don't know." She was still sitting there. He wished he could make out her expression.

"Would you feel better if you went and checked on her?" Clover asked.

"You wouldn't mind? After all, I'm here with you."

"Mace, ol' buddy, you haven't been with me from the moment I walked into the room. Go check on her."

He thought about denying her statement, but instead just got up and started for Zoe's table, and could have sworn he heard Clover mutter, "This should be interesting," but he wasn't sure and wasn't about to ask what she meant by it anyway.

Chapter Four

"Is everything all right, Zoe?"

Zoe wanted to moan. She had a raging headache and the last thing she needed was Mace Mason making it worse.

"Fine," she lied. "Just fine. I thought you were having dinner with Clover?"

"I am. We're over there." He pointed toward the other side of the restaurant. Clover waved when Zoe looked in her direction.

That would teach her not to check out the entire restaurant when she came in. But she'd spotted Rob right off and didn't need to check any further ... or so she'd thought.

"Well, great. Have a good time. I'll see you at the paper in the morning."

"Your date left," he said, ignoring her not-so-subtle hint he should leave.

"Rob wasn't my date, and yes, he did." *Thank you, Captain Obvious*, she thought, but didn't say.

"So now you're eating alone?"

She refused to answer his statement disguised as a question. Of course she was alone.

When she didn't say anything, he continued, "You could come join Clover and me."

"I don't think so. Three's a crowd and all that. I'll see you tomorrow though."

Mace didn't appear to get the hint. Instead of saying, *well goodnight then*, or even *see you in the morning*, he said, "I'm sure she'd love having you join us."

She pasted a smile on her face, sure that any reporter worth his salt would see how fake it was, then spoke slowly and clearly. "I don't think so, but thanks for the invitation. See you tomorrow."

"You still seem upset," he said, still not leaving.

Oh, what a brilliant, insightful man.

"I'm not," she assured him, even as she worried about straining a smile-muscle in her face.

"What's in the file?" he asked, an innocent lilt to his voice.

"Nothing. Just personal business between Rob and I." There was nothing incriminating in the file. Old articles on Hiho and notes from her conversations with Bertram— notes that contained questions on just what year Hiho was really founded in.

She didn't want Mace to see them and start digging around.

"You're sure about dinner?" he asked.

"Positive." Finally he understood at least that much. "But thanks for asking. Enjoy yourself and I'll see you in the morning." It was another dismissal, and she held her breath, waiting to see if he'd take the hint this time.

"Well, if you're sure," he said slowly.

She forced another smile. "Positive. Good night."

She let out her breath when he walked back to his dinner with Clover.

Zoe finished her coffee in two quick gulps, left money for Pete, and left the restaurant before Mace could come back and grill her some more.

What a night.

Rob didn't have much to say other than he wanted her to just drop the whole thing. No one had presented him with any proof that Hiho wasn't a hundred and he didn't want them to. He wanted to award the endowment to the college and the library this year.

He got mad when she pressed him.

Well, mad for Rob was sort of irked for the rest of the world, but it was the most worked up she'd ever seen him.

He didn't want to know. He'd made that clear.

No one in town wanted any proof brought to light.

Not that she blamed them.

She wasn't all that keen on bringing the information out in a public and un-ignore-able way either.

But first and foremost, she was a reporter. It was her job to simply present the facts. Morally, she felt she had to look into this.

Sometimes she hated having scruples.

"*Psst.*"

Zoe didn't even have to turn around to know who was *psst*ing her. "Bertram? Where are you?"

Though the street was well lit, the alley the *psst* had originated from was dark. The *psst*er was there, hidden in the shadows.

"Listen, I saw you talking to Rob," Bertram stage-whispered. "He doesn't want to know, does he?"

"No. He doesn't want to have to wait another year to give the college that money. They're counting on it."

"This isn't about wants, this is about the facts. We're reporters and we can't allow the facts to be covered up, even if we want to."

She stepped closer to the shadow and could make out Bertram's form, a slightly darker blob in a dark shadow. "I know. But Bertram, I don't have any facts, any proof."

"You'll find it." There was confidence in his tone. He believed in her abilities as a reporter.

"What if I don't want to?" she asked softly, voicing her private thoughts.

What if she didn't pursue this story? Would it make her less of a reporter?

"You're too good a reporter to just sit on this, Zoe. If there's proof, you'll find it and report it. I found that old letter in the newspaper's archives. They never ran the story in the Herald, so even back then no one wanted this truth to come out. Fool that I was, I turned the original over and didn't make a copy. I'm getting sort of slow in my old age. But you're on top of the game. You'll do better."

"I gave up *better* years ago and opted for happy," she murmured more to herself than to Bertram. She'd been thinking about that a lot since Mace arrived. When she'd left New York she'd left bigger and better behind and it had worked. She'd been happy ... until now.

Thinking about happy made her think about Mace, which made her head hurt worse than it had in the restaurant.

"And Zoe, I'm sure you'll be there looking for a solution when it comes out."

"But—"

"I've got to get back. I'll talk to you later." The dark blob shifted and she could hear the soft patter of footsteps moving away from her.

He was gone.

Zoe wasn't cut out for all this espionage stuff. She didn't want to investigate something that could ultimately hurt the community.

And yet, Bertram was right, she was too good a reporter not to.

Worry about the whole Centennial situation nagged at her all the way home.

Longer than that even.

She spent her night tossing and turning.

Sure, some of the tossing had to do with the whole Hiho problem, but a lot of it was Mace's fault. Every time she shut her eyes, there he was … kissing her.

Over and over again that night he kissed her.

And not on the cheek.

She'd wake up bound and determined not to fantasize about his kisses any more, and then … she'd start to wonder just how much she had to dig into the whole age of Hiho thing. And if she found the proof how she could keep it from hurting the college.

She'd worry about that until she dozed off again and there he'd be.

Kissing her.

Every time it looked like her dream Mace might go beyond kissing, she woke up.

Thank goodness.

She'd rather worry about Hiho than about Mace Mason kissing her.

Zoe finally gave up on sleep at about six, which was an ungodly hour, in her estimation.

Really, the only thing that should be up at six a.m. was … she couldn't think of anything that should be up that early.

But she couldn't face going back to sleep. She didn't want Mace invading her dreams one more time, so she got dressed and headed to the office. It wasn't as if she didn't have enough things that needed done. She'd use the extra hours to maybe get a bit ahead.

She ignored the fact that she felt tired. No, more than that, she felt haggard.

Worn and short-tempered.

It was all Mace's fault.

She made coffee and poured herself a huge mug. Because it was too early to start any of the hundreds of calls she had to make, she decided to do some digging through the paper's archives, looking for more proof.

Somewhere along the line she got lost in the research and forgot about Mace Mason.

"Zoe?"

Zoe almost jumped out of her chair at the sound of her name.

She didn't have to turn around and see who said it. She knew that voice. Had heard it whisper her name over and over again last night.

She whirled around. "Don't sneak up on me like that."

"I didn't sneak," Mace said. "I walked in. That bell on your door even jangled."

"Well, I didn't hear it." Wow, that sounded grumpy, but she didn't try to soften her words.

"Obviously." He held out a cardboard tray with a small bag balanced on it. "I have a peace offering."

She eyed it suspiciously. "What is it?"

Not that she figured he'd poison her.

"Aunt Aggie sent you one of her muffins." He handed her the bag.

Zoe couldn't help the muffled groan of anticipation as she took it. Aggie Watson's muffins were renowned in Hiho.

"And Pete assured me you had a fondness for French Vanilla Cappuccinos. Did he lie?" He shot her one of those one thousand kilowatt smiles. The type of smile designed to make women go weak in the knees.

Of course, his smile wasn't why her knees felt suspiciously weak. No. It was her state of utter exhaustion. Her sleepless night had weakened her.

But she did allow a small smile as she took the cup. "Thanks."

"You seemed a little short last night. I wasn't sure if I'd done something, so I thought a peace offering, just in case, was in order."

"Are you accustomed to annoying people and not knowing what you did?"

He shrugged. "It does seem to be a particular talent of mine."

She remembered she hated his shrugging tendencies and was thrilled to recall a flaw. Even if it wasn't much of one.

Feeling better, she said, "It wasn't you I was annoyed at last night."

No. It hadn't bothered her at all that Mace had dinner with Clover. She liked Clover and if Clover liked Mace … well, it might show a lack of taste on Clover's part, but it certainly didn't bother Zoe.

Nah. She didn't care who Mister-Big-City-Reporter dated.

She took a sip of the cappuccino, which tasted far better than her rather bitter coffee had. "But if I had been annoyed, I'd forgive you after the first sip. I wasn't, but thanks for the cappuccino."

"You're welcome."

"Now, about today. What do you want to do?"

"I thought I'd dig around in your archives, if you don't mind. I want to get a better feel for Hiram. After that, I was wondering if you'd take me on a tour of the town?"

"I have to go out to the fairgrounds later," she said, making it sound more like a statement than an invitation.

"I haven't been out there yet. Is it in walking distance?"

"Just about everything in Hiho is within walking distance. That's the way it was planned. Actually, Hiram had a vision for what he wanted this town to be, and keeping most of it within walking distance was part of it."

"So Hiram was one of the nation's first city design engineers?"

"Something like that. He was a man of vision and I think he's responsible for Hiho being the town it is now."

Mace nodded. "About last night."

"I thought we covered that. I wasn't mad about you dating Clover."

"Not that. You and Rob Pawley. You were discussing something, something that didn't make either of you happy. Care to tell me what?"

"I'm a reporter, too, remember," she said slowly. "I know when someone's fishing for a story. There's no story between Rob and me."

"I'm not fishing. I'm just observant. Something was up. That's fact, not conjecture."

"No," she insisted even though she knew she wasn't a very good liar, and though it was technically true that there was nothing between her and Rob, something was in fact up and it didn't take much of a reporter to sense that.

"Yes, there is," Mace said slowly. "And I suspect that the *psst*er the other day in the restaurant is part of it. Bertram. I bet it won't take much asking around to locate him. And when I do, I suspect he might be more forthcoming with answers than you are."

"Mace, there are no answers. Conjecture, but nothing solid enough for a story."

"So what's the conjecture?"

He wasn't going to let this go. He was like a dog that had grabbed hold of a bone and was going to gnaw it to death until he got some answers.

Deciding that it would be better to have him as an ally, than to have him as a opponent, Zoe decided to tell-all. Maybe having someone else working with her would help. After all, two pairs of eyes were better than one, especially if one pair of eyes were a dark chocolaty brown that...

Zoe shut off fantasies about Mace's eyes, shut off any stray fantasy of Mace himself.

"If I tell you," she said slowly, "do you promise not to report on anything without proof? Irrefutable, solid proof?"

"Zoe," he said, drawing her name out far beyond its two syllables. "I realize you don't know me very well, but I can guarantee you I'm not in the habit of running unsubstantiated stories."

"This story could really hurt the town—a town I love. I was looking for something to refute it this morning."

"Tell me what it is and I'll help you get to the bottom of it. You know what they say about two heads being better than one."

Zoe studied him a moment. Could she afford to trust him?

She wasn't sure. She just knew that she couldn't afford not to, at least not to trust in his journalistic integrity.

Trusting him for anything beyond that would be foolish.

And Zoe Wallace might be many things, but she wasn't foolish.

"Okay," she said, "here's what I know..."

❧ ❧ ❧

Mace listened as Zoe related the story of the Centennial that might not be.

At first he wanted to laugh. After all, the fact that Hiho, Ohio, a little podunk town in the middle of nowhere was ninety-nine, not one hundred wasn't much of a story. But as she went on and explained the financial ramifications a Centennial mix-up could have on the college's endowment…an endowment they'd already borrowed against, he began to see the issue in a different light.

"That's what I was talking to Rob about last night," she said.

Mace didn't want to reflect on the fact that he felt a surge of relief that she was out with Mr. Weak-Chin because of a story, and not because she was dating him.

"And what did…" He almost said *Mr. Weak-Chin*, but thought better of it. Zoe might misinterpret the comment and think it had something to do with jealousy, rather than a simple bit of brutally honest insight.

Instead he said, "…the lawyer have to say?"

"Rob's basically playing an ostrich, burying his head in the sand. He doesn't want to know. Doesn't want to have to hold off awarding the endowments until next year."

"But despite the fact he asked you to let it drop, you're going to investigate?" Mace asked.

"How can I just let it go? You might not think much about The Herald, though it's only a small weekly community paper, I've tried to make it the best paper it can possibly be. I'm a reporter. This is a story. Reporting it is what I do."

"So where do we start?" he asked.

She thumped one of the big bound volumes of back-issues on the table.

"I pulled out some of the oldest Heralds. Let's go see what they were writing about back then."

Mace's admiration of Zoe grew as the morning hours melted away in a haze of dusty old volumes of The Herald. She was intense in her perusal of the old papers.

He knew he wasn't nearly as focused. He kept stealing glances at her. She didn't even notice, but he noticed a lot of things.

He noticed that she chewed on her lip when she was concentrating.

It was cute.

Endearing even.

And thinking any woman was cute and endearing was enough to make him want to gag. Mace forced himself to get back to the task at hand and forget all about lip-chewing, cute, endearing Zoe Wallace.

After all, he was only in town a few more days.

Then he noticed that she twisted her hair on occasion. Just an absentminded little gesture. It made him want to reach out and simply touch her hair and see if it was as soft as it looked.

The urge was so strong that he folded his hands on his lap and tried to concentrate on the paper in front of him.

Nothing could come of this…attraction he felt for her. He had to remember that.

"…Listen to this," she said with a laugh. "*Mrs. Rose Caruthers hosted a tea today for the ladies of the Seventh Avenue Church.*"

She looked up, and he noted there was a smudge of dirt on her nose.

"They list her complete menu," she said. "Not exactly news, is it?"

Mace had an overwhelming desire to wipe the dirty smudge off for her. To take his finger and lightly trail it down the outline.

He firmly kept his hand in his lap. No way was he rubbing Zoe's dirty nose.

After yesterday's kiss, he planned to keep as far away from her physically as he could.

If a chaste little peck on the cheek could leave him fantasizing about more … well, it was best not to take any chances. After all, he was out of here first thing Monday morning.

He was so anxious to get back to Erie he planned to be up at the crack of dawn Monday and hit the road so he …

Mace lost track of what he was thinking as he stared at Zoe. She did look cute with her dirty nose, laughing over old menus.

"You know, I just had a great idea," she said, as she flipped through the book. "Each issue of The Herald, I could go back and find an old story, such as Mrs. Rose's tea menu and print it. I bet readers would love the look at our history. What do you think?"

He shrugged and she she went on, rambling about the new column, about possible ideas about …

He lost track of what she was saying. He was simply lost in her. She was, without a doubt, captivating.

A dirt smudge made him want to reach out and touch her, and he found her happy enthusiasm for her town attractive, what was happening to him?

He had no business thinking about Zoe that way.

They were opposites.

He loved the big city, he longed to advance his career, he was working toward bigger and better things.

Out of nowhere came Zoe's question.

What about happiness?

Why couldn't he shake that one small passing comment?

Of course he wanted happiness. But unlike Zoe, he didn't think a one-horse, podunk town was the magic elixir to all his frustration.

No, leaving WMAC was.

No more *nice news.*

Hard-hitting, meaningful stories, that's what he needed.

No, he had nothing in common with Zoe.

And that was that.

"Are you hungry?" he asked, needing to get out of this intimate isolation. Out in the real world he'd be more able to keep his thoughts on business. They had a story to chase down and they couldn't do that if they stayed hidden in this office, together... alone.

"Sure," she said. "I don't think there's anything in the paper itself."

"Let's give it a break. We'll get some food, then we'll walk out to the fairgrounds and I'll take some footage. We'll come back to the search later."

"Sounds great," she said.

It was a relief to get out of the office. They started walking down Main Street towards the restaurant.

"Tell me about this history thing you do," Zoe said as they walked.

Mace told her about Erie Chronicles, about the stories he'd covered, about how satisfying he found the work.

Satisfying.

Even as he said the word to her, he realized that he did find Chronicles fulfilling. That it was his favorite part of the job.

That one tiny facet of what he did made the rest of the job bearable.

What did that mean?

Steph had told him to spend this time figuring out what he wanted.

What did the Chronicles have to do with it?

"Mace?" Zoe said.

"Yes?"

"You just passed Pete's." She pointed to the window.

"Oh." The woman had him totally bemused. Why?

As the day passed he wasn't any closer to an answer. It was as if he was walking through a haze and everything was a bit of a blur. They ate, walked out to the fairgrounds. He got a bunch of footage of the town with Zoe narrating. Rather than do a voice over, he wondered if she'd consider being featured in the documentary part.

He wondered a lot about Zoe.

He should be wondering about the story, about the Centennial-that-possibly-wasn't.

But mainly, as the day progressed, he found himself wondering what it would be like to kiss her again? Kiss her for real.

What it would be like hold her?

What it would be like to ...

"Geesh, Mace. Stay with me here, okay?"

"What?" He gave himself a physical, as well as a mental shake.

"You keep drifting off," Zoe said.

"I never drift," he said quickly, probably too quickly. "I'm just thinking about the Centennial and Bertram's accusation."

"Me, too. I can't get it off my mind. Even when I was meeting with those venders, I was thinking about it."

"What if we grab a pizza and head back to your office? There has to be something more than a tea-party menu in those old papers."

"There's a lot about the incorporation, about the celebration when the town was official, but there's nothing the following year about messed up paper work."

"Maybe no one wanted it known," he said. "Just like no one wants it known now."

"Maybe," she admitted.

"Do you have any other records... not the papers, but other notes?" Mace asked.

"Yes. The paper has always been owned by pack rats. You can't believe the number of old boxes in the basement, all filled with old files. I keep two dehumidifiers running full time so that they don't rot. I keep swearing I'm going to go through them all, but have never had the time."

"So what do you say we make time tonight? Pizza and a treasure hunt?"

Zoe smiled and the sight hit Mace right in the gut.

"You're on," she said.

Off, not on.

He had to turn off all these wild fantasies about Zoe Wallace.

He had to turn them off hard and fast.

Hard and fast.

Wrong thing to tell himself, as it brought even more vivid pictures into his head.

He needed to think about something else. Something safe.

Food.

He was going to think about food, not about everything he'd like to do with Zoe.

"So what do you like on your pizza?" he asked.

Ah, now there was a safe subject. Pizza. You couldn't turn that into some hot mental image.

"Everything," Zoe said, oblivious to his raging fantasies. "I like everything."

Mace groaned, knowing he'd like everything, too.

Chapter Five

Zoe yawned for the fifteenth time.

She knew it was the fifteenth time because she was counting.

Even worse than that, she was sitting here thinking about yawning, in hopes she would yawn, because if she yawned it indicated she was bored, and if she was bored she couldn't possibly be interested in Mace.

But, as logical as the plan sounded, it wasn't working.

The man was driving her nuts in countless different ways. He worked with a drive that rivaled her own, something she was unaccustomed to. He had a killer smile and a great sense of humor that made her laugh one minute … the next he was annoying her so much she'd find herself gritting her teeth.

But mostly, despite the fact she didn't want to, he was driving her nuts because she wanted him.

Oh, not in a soul mate sort of way—she hadn't known him long enough for that—but rather in a strip-off-his-clothes-and-have-her-way-with-him sort of way.

She had to get away from him before she acted on her desire.

"Mace, maybe it's about time to go to bed," she said.

She groaned over her word choice and hastily added, "I mean, head home. Not that you have a home here. You don't. Your home is in Erie. But…well, what I mean is why don't you head back to Aunt Aggie's and I'll head back to my house and then we can both go to our own individual beds and get back to this tomorrow because I've done about all I can do tonight. Why, I've yawned fifteen times and—"

She yawned again just to prove she could. "See, I felt that sixteenth one coming on, and there it was. Anyone would have to agree that sixteen yawns indicate that you're tired, too tired for—

"Zoe?" Mace said interrupting her.

Zoe wasn't going to inform him that interrupting was poor form, but it was and she noted it with satisfaction. Just one more reason why she should not be attracted to Mace—he was rude.

Rudeness annoyed her.

And at this point she welcomed the fact that there was something else to be annoyed about.

"Yes?" she asked.

"You know you tend to rattle on about absolutely nothing when you're nervous. The question I have to ask myself is, *why is Zoe nervous?*"

"I can't imagine where you got that idea because I'm not nervous." The denial sounded weak even to her own ears.

It must have sounded just as weak to Mace's ears as well because he quirked an eyebrow at her. She found the whole crooked eyebrow thing sexy, so she glanced at his ears since ears were rarely sexy, but darned if Mace's ears weren't just as hot as the rest of him seemed to be.

She'd never thought about ears being attractive, but his were. Small, close to his head. They'd be fun to nibble on.

Oh, no, she was thinking about nibbling on Mace's ears?

Quickly, she tried to force another yawn, but couldn't quite manage it.

She realized Mace was talking, and forced herself to ignore his cute ears and listen to what he was saying. "…you definitely are nervous and the question is, why?"

"I'm tired. Not nervous. If you knew me better, you'd recognize the difference, but we've only known each other a couple of days, so of course you don't know me well enough to tell. So if I rattle on a bit—which I'm not admitting I do—but if I do, then it's only because I'm tired. Why, I've yawned fifteen times…sixteen now, isn't it? Why, that demonstrates being tired, not nervous."

There. She told him. She was so unaffected by his presence, that not only was she yawning, but she was counting those yawns.

"I don't think being tired is why you're rattling." He moved closer, just a fraction of an inch, but still, it was closer and closer wasn't what she wanted to be with Mace right now.

Okay, maybe closer was what she wanted, but it was what she should avoid.

"Then what possible reason would I have for yawning if it wasn't because I was tired?" She wished she could back away and put more distance between them, but she was up against the arm of the couch and had nowhere to move to.

"I wasn't talking about the yawning. I was talking about the way you're jabbering on and on about nothing. I think it's because you're nervous, and I think you're nervous because you're thinking what I'm thinking." He moved another fraction of an inch closer.

"And what are you thinking? Because I don't have a clue. Actually, I have a hard time figuring out what any man thinks. Maybe it's because their brains are wired differently than females. And females are ever so much more logical than males because of that wiring difference. And—"

"Take a breath, Zoe," he paused and added, "And move a little closer. Meet me in the middle and we'll see if we can figure out why you're nervous."

Zoe wasn't moving even one more inch closer to Mace. She wanted distance from him. She cursed herself for buying such a small sofa. She should have bought something bigger for the office.

Podunk.

Podunk.

Podunk.

She chanted his insulting description silently, hoping to get annoyed all over again with his big-city-superior attitude, but instead, she found herself sliding a tiny bit closer to him.

She was sure the slight movement was just the way the couch tilted, because she didn't want to want to be closer to Mace.

"A little closer," he prompted.

"What if I don't want to come closer?" she asked, hoping he'd say something really stupid and irritating so that moving closer to him would be the last thing she'd want to do, rather than the thing she yearned to do.

"You do," he said.

Do? Just what did she do? She'd lost track of the conversation and how on earth was she going to get irritated if she was losing track?

"My brain," he continued, "might be wired differently than yours, but I think you're thinking the same thing I am and if you move closer I'd like to do what we're both thinking about."

Oh, they were going to do what they'd both been thinking about. Not that she wanted to do that.

And she was pulling out a level and shimming the couch tomorrow so it wasn't so darned crooked. Why she was pretty sure she'd shifted a little closer because of the darned tilt.

"What do you think I'm thinking?" she practically croaked because she couldn't remember what she was thinking again. Mace must be practicing voodoo and wiping her thoughts out of her brain moments after she thought them.

Oh, no. She'd felt it for sure that time. She'd slid a tiny bit closer. Before she could move away, Mace pulled her toward him, eliminating the remaining space.

"I think you're thinking this," he said, his breath brushing softly against her cheek because she was that close. Too close.

Suddenly he was even closer, his lips pressing to hers.

It was a kiss. It was only a kiss.

She kept the words in her head, hoping to make herself believe it... but she didn't.

Podunk chanting didn't help either.

Maybe nothing was helping because the tender touch of his lips to hers was a total different species than *just a kiss.* It was Christmas and the Fourth of July all wrapped up in one—surprising and explosive.

It went on and on, until she forgot everything else but the feel of his lips on hers.

She forgot that Mace was leaving in a few days, that he thought her paper was podunk.

She forgot that her couch tilted.

She forgot that he wanted bigger and better, while all she wanted was happy.

The last part was easy to forget, because while they kissed, her body molded along his, she was indeed happy.

Content.

Excited.

When the kiss ended, she couldn't have said how long it had lasted. Maybe just seconds. Maybe minutes. Maybe a piece of eternity.

All she knew was it hadn't been long enough.

"That wasn't what I expected," Mace muttered.

"You said the same thing about my house," she felt the need to point out, hoping to annoy herself again, but she didn't feel annoyed, she felt surprisingly un-annoyed.

"I seem to say that a lot about you, Zoe." He stroked her hair. Just a small casual gesture, but even that was something to be treasured.

"Maybe that's your problem, Mace," she said.

"What do you mean?"

"You go into things with a preconceived notion. You thought I'd have an *Aunt Bee-ish* house. I didn't. You thought there couldn't be a story here in Hiho. There is. And you thought... I don't know what you thought about kissing me."

"Thinking about kissing you is all I've been able to think of for quite some time. Last night, when you were with that lawyer, I was crazy with thinking you might kiss him."

"Kiss Rob? Ew."

Robert Pawley was the vanilla pudding of mankind.

Now there was nothing wrong with vanilla pudding, if a person liked that sort of thing. But Zoe was pretty sure she preferred... what would she call Mace? He wasn't a dessert at all.

He was barbecued wings.

Not just plain old barbecued wings. No. The killer spicy variety that some restaurants served. Hot, spicy and just a bit dangerous to the brave souls who gave them a try.

"And how do you feel about kissing me?" he asked.

"I'll admit *ew* isn't the first word that comes to mind," she said.

"What word is?"

She wasn't sure he'd appreciate being compared to wings —barbequed or otherwise—so she settled for saying, "Confused. I don't normally...I mean, we've only known each other for such a short time and I don't..." She sighed. "Let's put it this way, *it's not what I expected.*"

He smiled, obviously understanding the joke, recognizing his own words being thrown back in his face.

"Well, now that we both know what to expect when we kiss, what do you say we do it again?" he asked.

"Mace, I don't know if we should."

"Zoe, you said I should concentrate on being happy, well, kissing you is about as close to being happy as I've been in a long time. I'd like to try it again and see if maybe I can get even happier."

She was moving toward him, knowing that smart or not, she was going to say yes.

But before she could get that one small word out and plant her lips on Mace's, she heard, "*Psst.*"

Mace turned, knowing who he'd find standing in the doorway. "Mr. Barky. Can we help you?"

Zoe scooted back across the couch to her own corner and looked like a girl whose father had just come in and caught her necking with a boyfriend.

"Bertram," she said, her voice a little higher than normal, "how did you get in here? I know I locked the door."

"I still have a key." He held a key ring aloft, jiggling it for affect. "Remember?"

Zoe gave a quiet little groan that Mace was pretty sure Bertram missed.

When she didn't say anything, Mace said, "So what can we do for you?"

"I came to see Zoe." There was a bit of antagonism in the man's voice.

More than a bit, as a matter of fact.

Mace didn't need to be a scholar on human nature in order to recognize that Mr. Barky wasn't pleased with the idea of him kissing Zoe.

If he was honest, Mace would have to admit, he wasn't so sure he was pleased either.

Not that he didn't enjoy kissing Zoe. He did.

A lot.

But kissing Zoe made him want to try other things…things that would be even more complicated. He was leaving first thing Monday morning and, despite what Zoe might think—and she did seem to be prone to thinking the worst of him—he wasn't in the habit of casual relations with a woman.

As a matter of fact, it wasn't that he wasn't in the habit of—he didn't have casual relationships, period.

"Well, I'm right here, Bertram. What can I do for you?"

"I see that. You're here late at night, with a practical stranger."

"Yes, she is," Mace said, with forced ease. "And I'm not quite a stranger any more, am I Zoe?"

She didn't answer, but Mace didn't really expect her to. She did however blush, which wasn't what he expected at all.

He felt a tiny bit smug about that hint of pink in his cheeks. He knew that the blush meant that she knew that they were more than just strangers. Exactly how to describe their relationship, he wasn't sure, but *more than strangers* was at the very least, accurate.

He smiled and continued, "We were looking for your evidence, Mr. Barky, but we haven't found anything."

"I don't think you'll find it in old newspapers. I've been over them with a fine-tooth comb. You'll notice there are issues missing from the archives. Maybe they got to them. But maybe they haven't got to the old files."

"I wonder who this *they* is," Mace muttered.

"Bertram," Zoe said, "We already realized that we weren't going to find anything in the archives and we're going to go through the old files tomorrow."

"And yet, you're both still here, sitting on the couch. Just what were you doing, eh?" He studied them both with a practiced stare.

Zoe's cheeks turned an even brighter shade of red, but she said, "Bertram, I don't think that's any of your business."

"I think you're wrong, Missy." Bertram waggled a finger in her face.

"*Missy?*" Zoe said, annoyance evident in her tone. "Now, see here, I'm an adult and I'm quite able to decide who I want to spend time with and—"

Bertram interrupted her. "I don't think so."

"Pardon me? I must have heard you wrong because I thought you said—"

"I don't think so," he repeated, interrupting her. "You wouldn't be the first woman to be taken in by a pretty face. And I'm afraid that's all this man is."

"Hey," Mace protested.

He was more than a pretty face. He was a reporter. An under-valued one perhaps, but a good one.

"Sorry. You seem like a nice enough guy, but you're not for our Zoe," Bertram said.

"Why do you say that?"

It wasn't as if Mace pictured himself settling down forever with Zoe Wallace, but it grated being dismissed out of hand like that.

"You've got the big-city itch all about you," Bertram said.

"What?"

"It's a restlessness. A need for the type of fast-paced world you'll never find here in Hiho."

Mace heard Zoe mutter, "*Bigger and better.*"

"How would you know?" Mace asked. "You don't know a thing about me."

Neither did Zoe, for that matter. Oh, she knew the feel of his lips pressed against hers now, but she didn't know him, despite her attempts to psychoanalyze him. And suddenly it struck him that he wanted her to know. He wanted to share things with her and he wasn't sure why.

"You'd be surprised," Bertram said. "I could tell you all sorts of autobiographical information. What college you attended—that first little station you worked for in New York after graduation—when you started working for WMAC. I could probably even guess at how frustrated you are with the current direction the station is taking with its news program. I suspect you're thinking about a move, but I can guarantee you're not thinking of moving in Hiho's direction. And since that's the case, if you and Zoe start something, she'll end up hurt."

"How could you know all that?" Mace asked.

"I was a reporter...and it's not something you retire from. It's in your blood. An itch you can never quite shake. I see something new, my first instinct is to explore it. I checked you out, Mace. You're a fine reporter. And I was very impressed with your Erie Chronicles, but you're not for Zoe."

"Bertram, you've been a good friend," Zoe said, "but that doesn't give you the right—"

"Zoe, your aunt—God rest her soul—was my best friend. It was always Zoe-this and Zoe-that. I knew you long before you took over the paper. And she'd have my hide if I didn't look out for you. So, like it or not, I'll say what you don't want to hear, don't mess with him," he jerked his head toward Mace. "You'll wind up hurt when he leaves."

"But—"

"And leaving is about the only thing you can count on from him," the old man said to Zoe.

"Bertram, I don't think you came to discuss me and Mace, did you?"

"No. I came to see if I could help, but since you don't want to see the truth about the town or the man, I guess it's time for me to go." He started toward the front door.

"Bertram, wait."

He turned. "What?"

"Walk me home, okay?"

"Zoe?" Mace asked. Now what was she thinking? "You don't have to go."

"Mace, Bertram's right. He's right about it being my duty as a reporter to find out the truth about Hiho's beginning and he's right about you and me. You'll be leaving when the Centennial Festival is over, looking for bigger and better. Me? I've found happiness in Hiho and I'm content with that. I'm pretty sure that even if being with you temporarily makes me even happier, in the long run, it will hurt me."

"You don't know that."

"But I do. Been there, done that, learned my lesson. I'll see you tomorrow bright and early for work...nothing else. Lock up when you leave, okay?"

Mace watched Bertram shepherd Zoe out the door.

It was probably for the best.

As much as he wanted Zoe, he had to admit that the odds were that he would indeed hurt her. After all, though he was looking to make a move from WMAC to something new, like Bertram said, he didn't think Hiho was quite the direction he'd be moving in.

He looked around the office. Zoe had mentioned boxes of old files in the basement. He might as well go have a look because chances of his getting any sleep tonight were slim to nil.

Hours later, countless boxes opened, searched then closed, Mace had found … nothing. He had the last box on his lap, with some of the oldest papers he'd found to date.

He pulled out a file but his eyes got heavy and he decided to just close them a moment before he took a look.

A moment turned into hours. There was light outside the basement window when he finally woke up from a dream … a dream starring Zoe Wallace, co-starring him.

Coffee.

He needed coffee to wake up and remove any lingering taste of Zoe from his mind.

He decided to take the file with him and go through it over at Pete's.

Zoe had been right when she said the small restaurant with the simple name would soon feel like home.

He'd settled into a booth and was leafing through the papers, coffee in hand, when a voice—a decidedly female voice—said, "What a morning. You wouldn't believe it. That darned new Sheriff gave me another ticket already. The man starts his rounds early just so he can ruin my morning. And speaking of mornings, you're up mighty early for a city slicker."

"Clover." Mace said. He felt a stab of guilt over how he'd treated her on their *date*. "About the other night—"

"Don't worry about it," she said, brushing away his apologies as she took the seat opposite him. "Sometimes the spark is there, sometimes it's not. So what are you doing?"

"Looking through old files from the Herald."

"What for?"

Mace wasn't sure if she'd heard about the Centennial that might not be, and he refused to start rumors, so he settled for saying, "Just looking for any information on the town and its beginnings. I'm not only covering the Centennial, but looking for information on Hiram for a short documentary series I do."

"If you want insights into the town's origins, I might be able to help."

"How?"

"There's always been a Clover in the family since the first Clover founded the college." She paused and added, "I know that's not going to help you. But the fact that the women in my family are notorious for keeping journals, just might. Big, long, extensive journals. And it just so happens I have a number of them that the first Clover wrote."

"Really? Do you think I could see them?"

She smiled. "I think that could be arranged. After you're done eating, stop over at The General Store. I'll have them for you."

"Thanks so much." He leaned across the table kissed her lightly on her cheek. He realized that he felt nothing over the kiss ... nothing like what he'd felt with a similar kiss with Zoe.

He didn't want to think about that. So he just said, "And thanks for understanding about the other night."

He was glad Clover understood him, because he certainly didn't understand himself. All he knew was that since the moment he saw Zoe Wallace and her bad makeover, she was all he could think about.

"Hey, I don't know if there's anything in them that will help. I don't think I've looked at them since I was in my teens."

"Well, I appreciate it no matter what they turn up."

CHAPTER SIX

Zoe breezed into Pete's Eats the next morning, firm in her resolve.

She was not kissing Mace again.

As a matter of fact, she felt a bit ashamed that she'd let last night's kiss bother to the extent that it had. Why, she'd practically run away afterward. You'd think she was a silly schoolgirl afraid of her first infatuation.

Infatuation.

It was a good word. It brought to mind something transitory, something that was just a passing fancy.

That's what Mace was—a passing fancy.

Oh, he was attractive enough, but he was just passing through, looking for something she wasn't sure he'd ever find. When someone was counting on *more* to make them feel fulfilled, it rarely ended well. There didn't tend to be enough *more* to ever satisfy anyone.

She'd learned that the hard way.

She felt a wave of sadness that he wasn't looking for happy. Mace Mason was a man who should be happy.

She cleared her thoughts again.

His happiness wasn't her concern.

Her own was. And she was going to be happy not kissing Mace Mason if it killed her.

Pasting a smile on her face, she called, "Hey, Pete."

"Hey, Zoe."

"Have you seen Mace?"

"Sure. Me and half the town," he snickered. "He was in here a bit ago, kissing Clover and making plans to meet up with her."

"Kissing Clover?" she repeated, not because she cared. Why, he was a legal, free adult and could kiss whomever he wanted to.

"Sure. The two of them stood there, bold as brass and he kissed her."

Podunk.

Podunk.

Podunk, Zoe chanted, just to remind herself that Mace was an annoying, annoying, small-town-biased man. Why she didn't care even the tiniest little bit who he kissed…

She realized that she was lying to herself.

The fink.

He kissed her last night and this morning he was kissing Clover.

Oh, he'd shown his true colors. And more power to him. Maybe he'd give up on bigger and better, and simply decided to concentrate on sheer quantity.

"He said he was heading over to Clover's when he finished his breakfast."

"Well, that's great. If he's with Clover I don't have to worry about him. I've got a thousand and one things to take care of today before the dinner."

Just great.

She didn't care who Mace Mason was kissing.

As long as it wasn't her.

Because she definitely didn't want to be kissing him again. As a matter of fact, she wasn't going to see him any more than she absolutely had to. Not because she was hurt

that he'd kissed Clover, but because she was busy. Too busy
to put up with his shenanigans.

She was rather proud of the fact that she was true to her
word and managed to avoid Mace all day.

Not that it was very hard.

She didn't see hide or hair of him, so avoiding him was
actually downright easy.

He was probably kissing Clover right now.

And she hardly even minded when she thought about it.
Not that she thought about it all that much. Why she'd man-
aged to go as long as ten minutes once without thinking of
Mace at all.

On one of those rare occasions when she had thought of
him, she realized she didn't even like him. Kissing him last
night had been the result of a sleep-deprived system. She
did a lot of crazy things when she was tired.

Why, in college, after cramming for finals, she was so
sleep deprived that she went to a karaoke bar and sang
Feelings.

Feelings!

Only the truly judgment impaired would sing *Feelings* to
a crowded bar ... or kiss Mace Mason.

As a matter of fact, she was glad he'd been absent all
day. She'd got a ton of work done. She had just enough time
to go home and get ready for the big dinner tonight at the
college.

Tomorrow the Festival started and she'd be run ragged
until it ended with the fireworks on Sunday.

Talk about sleep-deprived.

She'd better make it a point to stay away from karaoke machines and Mace Mason. That way, even if she did
have a sleep-deprived-judgment-impairment moment, she

wouldn't have to worry about making a fool of herself by singing … or kissing.

Yeah, that was for the best.

She let herself into her house and waited for the wave of ease that generally swept over her when she entered.

The only wave she got was a wave of annoyance when she realized her flowers were wilted and she hadn't thought to pick up another bunch.

She took the vase into the kitchen and tossed the flowers into the compost bucket. As she walked back through the living room it looked cold without the normal splash of color that lent the decor its drama and focal point.

Cold and almost clinical.

She didn't like it.

Even her house felt off-kilter since Mace arrived.

Thank goodness he was leaving Monday morning.

She'd just stepped out of the shower when she heard the doorbell. Wrapping her bathrobe around her, she padded barefoot to answer it.

She peeked through the peephole and her heart gave a small leap when she saw Mace.

She willed her heart back into its normal position.

Darn. He'd found her. So much for her avoiding abilities.

He knocked again. Through the peephole, his nose looked rather bulbous and distorted, but even the distortion couldn't disguise his impatience.

He knocked louder. "Zoe, I know you're in there. I saw your neighbor, the older lady with the garden. She said you'd just got home."

In New York she could come and go at will and no one ever noticed, but here, everyone knew everything. That was the one big downfall to small town life. Not that she'd admit there was anything negative about small town living to Mace.

"Yes?" she called through the door.

"Are you ready?" he called back.

"Ready for what?" *More kissing?* she wanted to ask, but didn't. Because she wasn't. And wouldn't. Ever.

"Ready for the party."

Of course, he wasn't talking about kissing. He was kissing Clover now.

"Oh, the party." She looked down at her bathrobe and clutched it a little tighter. "No, I'm not. I figured you'd be going with Clover."

"Now why would you—" he stopped, and said, "Zoe, it's ridiculous talking through the door. Are you going to let me in?"

"I just got out of the shower."

Her robe was thin. Why hadn't she noticed that before now? No way was she letting Mace in when the only thing that covered her was a threadbare bathrobe.

"So, unlock the door and I'll wait out here and count to twenty before I come in."

"I wasn't expecting you," she said.

"I don't see why. We'd talked about going together."

"But…" She couldn't think of an argument for not opening the door.

"Are you going to let me in?" he called. She looked through the peephole one more time and studied his big, flaring nose. She'd remember the way it looked and any thoughts of kissing Mace would evaporate instantly. Why it would work better than chanting *podunk*, which hadn't worked well at all.

"Yes." She fumbled with the locks. "Count to fifty before you open it."

"Okay."

Zoe rushed back to the bathroom. She closed and locked the door and rushed through dressing, uneasy, knowing Mace was somewhere lurking in her house.

Lurking.

Yeah. Thinking of Mace lurking was good.

It sounded ominous. Sinister even.

And that was better than kissable.

She toweled her hair and hurried through drying it. A light touch of makeup and she was done.

She remembered when she lived in New York, the idea of getting dressed to go out in under an hour would have appalled her, getting ready in under ten minutes would have totally mystified her.

But she looked in the mirror and was pleased with the affect.

She enjoyed the feeling because she was sure it wouldn't last. She had to deal with Mace, and dealing with Mace never left her feeling pleased.

Aggravated.

Annoyed.

Antsy.

Those were just the A's. She could probably go through the entire alphabet describing how Mace made her feel and never use the word *pleased*.

"Now, about the party," she started to say when she walked in the room.

Mace turned and let out a long whistle. "You look good."

"Uh, thanks. You look all right as well," she said because she didn't know what else to say.

That was the biggest understatement she'd ever made.

All right didn't even begin to cover how Mace looked in his suit. He looked like eye-candy.

Eye-candy who was toying with her.

Toying with her and Clover.

Remembering about him kissing Clover made her feel better.

"About the party—" she started to say, but Mace interrupted her.

"Where are the flowers?" he asked.

"What?" she asked.

"Last time, you had flowers on the table. They really stood out because of all the white, which is probably the only reason I noticed them. Noticing flowers isn't something I normally do. Or decor. I'm not the kind of guy who notices things like that, but you couldn't miss how white this room is, so of course, that made me notice the flowers. Where are they?"

"Well, thank you for clearing up your manly disinterest in interior design and flowers."

"So, where are they?" he pressed.

"I didn't have time to get any. I've been busy trying to run a business and get everything ready for tomorrow."

"And is it?" he asked.

"Is what?"

Zoe was lost. Normally she could follow a conversation no matter how many zigs or zags it took, but Mace was zigging way too much and looked way too good in his suit, which made her mind zag in uncomfortable directions.

"Is everything ready for tomorrow?" he asked.

"As ready as I can make it."

"Good. Then let's go." He started toward the door.

"About that, like I said, I figured you'd be going with Clover and made plans accordingly. You don't have to feel obligated to take me."

"Obligated?" he said as if it were a foreign word. "Is that how you think I feel?"

"Sure. You're dating Clover, kissing her in public, so of course you'd rather take her."

Darn. She wished she could take back that last part of her sentence—the kissing Clover part. She had planned on not mentioning the kissing Clover part to show him she didn't care, because of course, she didn't care.

"Kissing her? I never…" he hesitated and then started laughing. "Oh, that little peck on the cheek I gave her this morning? Is that what you're referring to?"

"I'm not referring to anything, I'm just saying, you're welcome to take her to the party tonight. I can manage myself."

"What if I told you that it was just a friendly little kiss. She'd gave me a new lead. The kiss—no, not kiss—the peck was just a thanks."

"If that's how you thank women for giving you information, what do you do when someone gives you something really important?"

"You know what, Zoe, you sound a bit…" he paused, and looked as if he was searching for the right word, then smiled as he continued, "jealous. Yes, jealous would be the word I'd use to describe how you're acting."

"Jealous?" Zoe scoffed. A loud, barky sort of scoffing sound. "Me, jealous? Of what? You?"

"Of me kissing Clover."

"You've got to be kidding." She snorted. She was proud of that snort. She felt it showed just the right amount of incredulity.

"Are you sure you're not upset about thinking that I've been kissing another woman?" he asked.

"Positive. There are things I'm absolutely positive of. I'm positive that the moon orbits the earth, just as the earth orbits the sun. I'm certain that I don't like brussel sprouts or liver. And I'm certain that there's no way I could ever be jealous of you kissing anyone."

There she'd told him.

Of course, maybe she felt the slightest twinge of something in the pit of her stomach every time she thought about Mace and Clover together. So it was a good thing for her that she didn't think of them often.

Hardly at all.

Why, the picture of Clover clinging to Mace, locked in his embrace rarely flitted through her mind.

"Well, if you're sure," he said, sounding skeptical.

"Totally sure. Why if I was any surer, I could…" She couldn't think of a single thing to say. What a stupid comment. She wasn't someone who was prone to stupid comments and the fact that she was making them now was just one more sin to pin on Mace.

"Well, since you're that sure, I won't worry about it. Let's go."

"Go where?" she asked, confused again.

"To the party."

She shrugged her shoulders, just to remind herself of his annoying shoulder-shrugging habit. "Whatever."

"Ah, don't be so enthusiastic, Zoe. You're embarrassing me."

"You think you're funny," she said, hoping she added just the right inflection to let him know she didn't think he was.

"I know I am."

She couldn't think of any brilliant retort, so she said, "So did you find anything?"

"Switching gears again," Mace said with a *tsk*.

The *tsk* was almost as annoying as his shoulder shrugging. She wished he'd tsk her again. But instead, he asked, "Find anything about what?"

"About Hiho's true centennial date."

"I still have some more research. But I don't want to talk about it tonight."

He was hiding something. She was reporter enough to recognize the evasion.

"If you found something and are holding out on me ..." she left the threat hanging, hoping it sounded ominous.

"Zoe, there's nothing I'd hold out on you. As a matter of fact, you're welcome to hold everything I have." He wiggled his eyebrows suggestively, a huge grin pasted on his very handsome face.

She stood up straight and looked him right in the eyes. "I don't think so."

Looking in his eyes was a mistake. She hadn't reckoned on how dreamy they were. Dreamy and captivating.

Darn.

"Your loss," he said with a grin and a shrug.

He whistled as she closed up the house and they headed out the door without another word.

He car was parked in her driveway. "I know you're fond of walking, but I thought we'd ride tonight."

"I normally just walk because it's faster than worrying about parking spaces when you're only going a couple blocks. But I do own a car and have been known to ride in one."

"Glad to hear it."

Zoe might not mind riding in cars, but she didn't want to ride in Mace's. She stood there, wondering how to get out of it without him starting on his you-want-me refrain again.

"Are you getting in?" he asked.

"I was just thinking that it might be better if I took my car. That way if I'm ready to go and you're still having a good time, you don't have to worry about me and vice versa."

"That's not what you're thinking. You're thinking that if I meet up with Clover I'll be free to leave with her."

He was wrong, but she let it slide and gave a noncommittal shrug.

"What do I have to say to get it through your thick skull that I'm not interested in Clover Addison?" He moved away from the car and toward her.

"Nothing," she said, taking a step away, keeping a nice bit of distance between them. "I mean, my skull's not thick and it doesn't matter if you're interested in her."

"I think it does." His voice was low and silky.

Zoe swallowed hard. "Are we back to that jealous thing again?"

"Yes."

"No."

"No?" he asked.

"No, I'm not jealous. And you don't have to convince me that you and Clover aren't an item because it doesn't matter," she said.

"I think it does and I think I do."

"Forget it."

"Come here." He didn't wait for her to move toward him. For a big man he moved fast. He closed the space that separated them in the blink of an eye.

Zoe knew what was coming. She could have turned away. Could have run screaming in the other direction. But instead she waited, wanting him to kiss her.

She'd thought last night's kiss was powerful, but this one…

It was the sucker punch of kisses.

Last night's kiss, which she'd thought was so hot, was in reality vanilla pudding and tonight's kiss was the barbecued wings.

"Wow," he muttered when he finally broke it off.

He broke it off because Zoe couldn't have, just like she couldn't run from the kiss.

The truth was, she was addicted to Mace Mason's kisses.

But that didn't mean she liked him.

And it certainly didn't mean she was jealous of Clover.

She brushed off her skirt and tried to adopt a blasé look as she said, "Let's go."

It just might have worked except her voice was breathy, as if she'd just run a marathon instead of having kissed a man.

Darn.

This was going to be the longest party ever.

Mace had met half of Hiho's population, he was sure.

He'd met the librarian, Katy Sloane, who'd given up her reign as Miss Hiho. He'd met Brandi, the runner up who was now the reigning Miss Hiho. He'd met Joel Carter and his Boss, Big Bert. He'd met the Mayor, a cute will-o-the-wisp woman named Victoria Robertson. She was petite and extremely beautiful, but he'd hardly given her a second look.

That was Zoe's fault.

He should be flirting with the cute little mayor.

Or even flirting with Clover.

Clover was a beautiful lady. Beautiful and not nearly as complicated as little Miss Don't-Kiss-Me, I'm-Not-Jealous Zoe Wallace.

Zoe was jealous. He was sure of it.

Well, pretty sure.

She'd been thinking about him and Clover all day and it was driving her nuts.

Good.

Turn about was fair play. She'd been driving him nuts since he left last night.

This whole town was driving him nuts.

He thought of the journal he'd read that afternoon.

That first Clover had a wonderful, candid writing style and a frank portrayal of her town. It had given him insights into Hiram Hump, which would make portraying the three-dimensional man ever so much easier.

There had also been a lot about Hiram's wife, Hortense.

Clover wrote about tutoring Hortense. The woman could read, but complained that the words seemed to move around right in front of her eyes.

Mace suspected that today she would be diagnosed with dyslexia. But back then … well, Clover had written that Hiram referred to his wife as *addlepated.* Clover had noted that he'd always said it with a smile of affection.

Affection.

That was the word she'd used to describe the Hump's relationship. And that affection was what led Hiram to come to Clover after he'd discovered that there had been a mix-up in the paperwork to incorporate the town.

Clover had fixed it and the town had been official in February of 1919. Not May of 1918.

Bertram was right. Hiho wasn't a hundred.

It was ninety-nine.

Mace looked at the crowd.

He spotted Aunt Aggie and Pete.

There was Clover, talking to the Mayor.

And Zoe? He scanned the room.

There she was talking to the infamous Mrs. Pete, the woman who injected such terror into Bertram and Pete's hearts, and could cook with the skill of an angel.

If he let this information out, he'd hurt all of them. The college would lose its endowment until next year. An endowment it had already borrowed against. He wasn't sure if they could put off payments that long. What would that kind of financial hardship do to the small, private college? And if something happened to the college, what would happen to the town?

Mace knew he couldn't sit on the information, as much as he wanted to protect Hiho and its residents.

Despite himself, he'd begun to like them all.

"Ah, you're that reporter boy that's been mooning over Zoe."

"Pardon?" Mace saw a small, older lady standing at his side. He knew he'd met her, but he couldn't quite place her.

"Cora. Cora Macintosh."

He nodded. "Ah, yes, the pie judging scandal."

"Are you mocking me, boy?" There was more than a hint of reprimand in her voice.

"No, ma'am, of course I'm not."

"I realize a small town pie competition might not seem all that important to you, but my sister and I take great pride in our cooking."

"I'm sure you do. Truly, I wasn't making fun of you."

He remembered when he'd talked to Steph right after he'd heard about the toothless judge. He had been making fun of the Macintosh sisters' concerns.

He felt a wave of shame.

"See to it that you don't." She waggled her finger in a way that made Mace wonder if she'd been a teacher once upon a time.

"Now, about your attraction to our Zoe," she continued.

"What?" he asked.

"You heard me. Everyone's noticed and is talking about it."

"Everyone in this town is out of their ever-lovin' minds if they think there's anything between me and Zoe." Even to his own ears his denial sounded less than forceful.

"Really? Well, let's see, there's the fact you two spent the night together—"

"In her office working. It was as platonic as can be." Well, practically platonic. One kiss didn't un-platonic it.

As if she'd read his mind, Cora said, "I don't call kissing platonic. And you did in fact kiss Zoe before you came here."

"How on earth do you know that?" It had only been, what, a half hour? How on earth did this woman know?

"Well, Lani Standish lives across the street from Zoe. She's been Zoe's aunt's neighbor for years…you did know that Zoe's house belonged to her aunt, right? Not that Zoe left it as a memorial to Betty. Zoe made it her own, though I don't know what she was thinking when she made that room all white. Why, imagine when she has children one day what they'll do to a white room. And it's sort of cold."

Mace wasn't about to argue that rather than cold the room was inviting, although the absence of flowers today bothered him. Zoe had said she was busy, but somehow he wasn't buying that explanation.

"…and so Lani told Bertram, who said that you'd spent last night at Zoe's, so kissing made sense, even if it didn't make any of us happy. And that's when I decided it was my duty to tell you to be careful. If you hurt our Zoe we'll hunt you down."

"Ah, just who is the *we* that will be hunting me?" Mace asked, not overly intimidated by the woman. As a matter of fact, he was touched that she was looking after Zoe.

From the sounds of it, half the town was looking after Zoe.

Mace tried to think of anyone in his life who would defend him with such vehemence, but he couldn't think of anyone. Oh, he was friendly with his colleagues and had a waving relationship with his neighbors, but there wasn't the connection that this small community seemed to have.

Mace knew the blame was his. He was so focused on his work that he rarely took time to concentrate on the people who surrounded him. Maybe that's why people were telling Stephanie he was terse.

Maybe he was.

"Ma'am, I assure you that I don't intend to hurt Zoe."

"And you know what they say about good intentions paving the road to hell, don't you?"

"I—"

"Mace, there you are. I want you to meet Rob Pawley," Zoe said, rushing in to save the day.

Mace waited to see if Cora was going to warn Zoe as well. But the older lady simply smiled and said, "Zoe, I was just getting to know your Mr. Mason."

"He's not my anything," Zoe replied quickly. Too quickly.

Cora shot Mace a look that said, *let's keep it that way,* and then started talking to Zoe.

Mace turned to the weak-chinned Rob Pawley. "I had hoped to have a chance to talk to you tonight. I understand you're in charge of the Pawley endowment."

"Yes. And I understand you're digging into this whole alleged Centennial mix-up. Don't."

"I'm a reporter," Mace said. "Digging is what I do. And even if I don't like what I find, I have to report it."

"Even if what you find is going to hurt a lot of people. The whole community?" Rob Pawley asked, echoing Mace's own concerns.

"So you believe that the town doesn't really turn one hundred until next year?" Mace asked.

"I'm not saying that," the weak-chinned man said hastily. "I've seen no tangible proof, just a lot of accusations."

Mace could show him written documentation, but he didn't say so, instead he said, "Is it possible for me to see the actual paperwork for the endowment?"

"See it?" Pawley echoed.

"The paperwork."

"The original document is old and fragile," he said slowly.

"A copy is fine. I just want to read it for myself."

Mace could see that Pawley wasn't pleased with the request, but the man gave him a curt nod. "Come to my office Monday and I'll get you a copy."

"I leave town on Monday." With the way news circulated in this town, Mace was sure the man knew that. Heck, he probably had heard about the whole kissing-Zoe thing as well.

"Is there any chance you could get it for me tomorrow?" Mace asked.

"I don't normally have office hours on Saturdays." Pawley sighed. "But I had to go in and do a few things, so I guess I could. Why don't you stop by about eight, if that's not too early."

"No, that's fine."

Someone across the room called Pawley. He turned and said, "I'll see you in the morning then, Mr. Mason."

Mace wasn't sure why he wanted to see the document. But when he did a job he tried to be complete and the endowment was the crux of the entire matter. If it wasn't for the endowment, the fact that the Centennial Celebration was a year off wouldn't matter.

But it did matter.

It mattered a lot to the whole town.

It mattered to Zoe.

And because of that, it mattered to Mace.

CHAPTER SEVEN

"I'm so glad that's over," Zoe said as they pulled in her driveway three hours later.

"You didn't enjoy yourself?" Mace asked.

"It was a bit too formal for my taste." Zoe didn't want to add that she'd spent the better part of the evening watching Mace, sure that he'd gravitate to Clover.

But strangely enough, other than a brief greeting the two hardly spoke. And they certainly hadn't kissed.

She had to stop thinking about Mace and kissing…whether she was thinking about him kissing Clover or kissing her.

She might not like the thought, but she certainly liked the kisses. Even though she wasn't sure she liked Mace.

Oh, he'd seemed like a nice guy, at first. After all, he hadn't laughed at her disastrous makeover.

But then there was the whole *podunk* thing.

And the fact that he was driven to succeed with no thought at all about happiness.

Plus, just for good measure, there was the stone-hard fact that he was leaving Monday.

Yes, she certainly should keep her distance from Mace.

And yet, when he turned off the car and walked her to the door, rather than bolting in the house and shutting the door in his face, she heard herself ask, "Would you like to come in for a drink?"

"No," was his flat response.

"Oh." Maybe she'd been mistaken, thinking that Mace was as attracted to her as she was to him. She opened the door and started inside.

"But," Mace said, gently holding her shoulder, "I'd like to come in and pick up where we left off earlier."

"And where was that?"

"I'd show you, but your neighbor, Loni Something—"

"Lani?" Zoe asked, not sure what he was talking about.

What had the snoopy old lady done now? It wasn't that she didn't like Lani, but the woman knew everything that happened on the block…knew it, and publicized it with an efficiency that rivaled the paper's.

"Seems she likes watching out her window and reporting our kisses to the whole town."

"Oh, no." She should have known better than doing anything in her front yard that she didn't want the entire town hearing about.

"Oh, yes. I've been warned to keep my distance or else I'm to be a target for a town-wide manhunt."

"Who said that?"

Zoe loved Hiho, loved being part of a community that looked after its own, but there was a difference between looking after and butting in.

"It doesn't matter. Part of me agrees with them. I should just walk away and forget how attracted I am to you." He stepped closer.

Zoe could smell whatever aftershave he used. Hot and spicy. The thought made her think of barbequed wings and she couldn't help but smile. "And the other part?"

"Wants you to follow you into the house and pick up where we left off earlier."

"This is probably a mistake," she said, knowing that that was a vast understatement, "but I think I agree with that second part."

"You do?" He sounded as surprised at her confession as she felt.

"Yes. I don't know why. You make me crazy. I think you've got your priorities all wrong and I know you'll be leaving Monday. And yet none of that matters." She opened the door. "I want you to come in."

They both entered the house and Zoe shut the door with a bang. Closing them away from Lani's prying eyes.

Closing the door on her doubts.

"And now…" She stepped into his arms and it felt like coming home. Worries slipped away. Thought as well. All that was left was feeling. A feeling of rightness. Of something more than that…

His lips lowered and met her anxious ones.

The sweet kiss went on forever.

And ever.

Sweetness gave way to need…more than need, urgency.

Zoe was the one who broke off the kiss. She ran her fingers through his hair, toying with it. "I need to tell you that I don't…I mean, we've only known each other such a short time and during that time you've annoyed me as often as you've delighted me. This…whatever it is, well, it's different than anything I've ever felt. I know you're leaving and I know this can't last, but none of that alters the fact that I want you. Want you more than I've ever wanted anyone."

"I can't make you any promises," Mace said softly.

"I know. That's why I'm not asking for any. I just want…"

Zoe made her living with words, using them to explain things. But this once, words failed her. She couldn't explain this to Mace, mainly because she couldn't explain the powerful feelings she had toward him to herself.

So she abandoned words and simply took his hand, leading him toward her bedroom.

"Are you sure?" he asked.

"Sh," she said.

She opened the door and drew him inside, closing it behind them.

Zoe woke and lay perfectly still for a moment, replaying the night before.

She wasn't a total innocent, but what she'd done with Mace was completely out of her scope of experience. She wasn't a one-night-stand sort of woman.

She wasn't even a short-term relationship sort of woman.

And yet with Mace, she couldn't help herself.

She rolled, ready to let him delight her again, and realized the bed was empty.

Her heart sank and she felt cold.

He'd left.

After their amazing night he'd left without even a goodbye.

She flopped back on her pillow, then realized there was a faint rumbling noise coming from outside her bedroom. A noise that wasn't a normal house noise.

He was still here.

Her heart sped up and she smiled as she climbed out of bed and tossed on her robe. She ran into the bathroom and took the quickest shower in the history of showers. She wanted to be with Mace, wanted to bring him back to her bedroom and have her way with him again.

Then she remembered today was the Centennial Celebration.

Darn.

Well, maybe tonight when it was over, he'd come back to her house with her.

She wrapped a robe around herself, not wanting to wait to dress to see him again. To reassure herself that he was indeed still here.

He was in the living room, looking out the window, a cell phone to his ear. "...yes, I got it, but I was busy...You were right, there is a story here. A newsworthy story even...It has to do with a centennial that wasn't...No, I'm not ready to do a spot on it. I still have a few facts to get straight...Yes...The History Channel?"

Mace was silent for a long time, listening to whatever whoever was saying.

Zoe hugged her robe tighter.

Aunt Betty used to say you never heard anything good when you eavesdropped.

That might seem like an odd sentiment for a reporter to have, but Aunt Betty wasn't the type of reporter to get her stories on the sly. She was up-front and honest in all her dealings.

Unlike Mace the-ratfink Mason.

He was going to run with the centennial that wasn't story.

Had he found some proof?

Probably. Zoe doubted he'd print the story if he hadn't.

He was going to lose the college and library their endowments and in so doing, hurt the community that she loved.

But Zoe could have forgiven that. Mace was a reporter after all, and reporting was his job.

But he'd held out on her.

She was sure he had proof... proof he hadn't shared.

She thought they were closer than that.

Oh, she didn't expect words of undying love, but even before last night, even when they fought, she'd thought they'd had a connection. A friendship even.

She'd trusted him.

Back in her New York days she would have known better than to trust another reporter with a big story. New York had been a dog-eat-dog, watch-your-back-at-all-times sort of atmosphere.

But here in Hiho, she'd learned to let down her guard.

That was her mistake.

Letting down her guard with Mace both professionally, and more importantly, personally.

The creep had double-crossed her.

"...What's to think about?" he said. "My future...Yes, I realize it's an opportunity of a lifetime, but I need to be sure it would be a lifetime I could live with, that I could be happy with...Yes. Monday morning. Bye. And Steph? Thanks."

He flipped his cell-phone closed.

Zoe stepped into the living room.

Mace smiled. "Good morning."

He took a few steps toward her, but Zoe countered his every step with one of her own, keeping distance between them.

"Don't good morning me, you fink."

He stopped in his tracks. "Zoe, after last night, I thought I'd warrant at least a good morning before we started fighting again. What did I do this time?"

"You have something about the centennial, something you didn't share."

He raked his fingers through his hair, and Zoe could almost feel the texture of it, feel the urge to plunge her own fingers into it, to tangle them up with his, to ...

No.

She was done lusting after Mace the-ratfink Mason.

He nodded. "You're right. I should have shared that, I want to fix whatever you're annoyed with and take you back to bed and—"

Zoe interrupted. "Don't play games with me, Mason. You have some proof about the centennial."

"Yes, I do," he said with a slight frown. "I was going to tell you."

"When? After the story was headlined on your show?"

Zoe couldn't believe she'd been taken in, that she'd fallen for Mace Mason's good-looking facade and hadn't seen past it to the ratfink underneath.

"I—"

She interrupted, not being in the mood for excuses. "Or better yet, were you going to wait until Rob was presenting the endowment checks to Leonard Stanley and Katy Sloane then drop your bombshell? Ah, that would make for a good sense of the dramatic. Why, you could even get it on tape, I imagine. It would make for a good news segment. More news than the non-news stuff you said you hated reporting."

"Zoe, do you really think I'd do that?"

He sounded ... hurt.

But Zoe wasn't going to be taken in again. She wasn't going to believe his act this time, nor was she going to believe the small tug coming from somewhere in the vicinity of her heart—a small tug that whispered Mace wasn't a fink. He was special.

Ha.

A special sort of fink, that's what he was.

"Listening to you made me realize I don't know you at all," Zoe said. "I thought I did. I thought I could trust this feeling I had for you, even though I only met you at the beginning of the week. I thought maybe that at-first-sight stuff was right."

"Love at first sight?" he murmured.

"I didn't say that *L* word. If I'd used an *L* word at all it would have been lust-at-first-sight. Maybe even friendship, but not love."

"So, do you go to bed with everyone you lust after?" he asked.

"Of course not," Zoe said.

He stepped closer, but this time she didn't move backwards, she held her ground.

"How about friends?" Mace asked. "Do you sleep with all your friends?"

"Don't be ridiculous and insulting. I told you that I don't normally do things like this."

"Then why me?"

That was the question. Why him? Something different than just friendship, than just lust whispered again, but she pushed the thought away. No matter what it was, she was done with Mace Mason.

"I don't know," she said. "But the point is, I didn't know you the way I thought I did. You're a fink. You used me."

"I used you?" he asked. There was a soft, dangerous quality to his tone that she'd never heard before.

"Yes. You used me to get the story. I didn't expect you to sit on the story if you found proof, but I told you about the situation assuming we'd share not only the looking for answers, but the finding of them. Once upon a time I would have known better."

"Zoe." His voice was sharp with censure.

Zoe felt a spurt of guilt, as if she was the one who'd done something wrong. But she knew she wasn't. The one who'd done wrong was ratfink Mace Mason.

"Get out, Mace. It's time for you to go. I have to get ready for the Parade and the Festival."

"Do you want to know what I'm going to do with the information?"

"No," she said. "You wanted the story so bad, it's yours. You run with it. And when you're done, I hope you run home to Erie and forget all about Hiho and about me, because I plan to do my best to forget about you."

"Zoe, I—"

She interrupted him. "Goodbye, Mace. Thanks for reminding me why I moved here. I'd almost forgotten what it was like before I came to Hiho, the looking over my shoulder, not truly trusting anyone. You go get your bigger and better life, and I'll stay here and settle for happy."

"I—"

"I don't have time for this. Goodbye, Mace."

She turned and walked away from him, walked away from the man she hadn't just lusted over, hadn't just felt friendship for.

Zoe was afraid she'd finally figured out just what it was she felt for Mace. She was very much afraid that she'd done the unthinkable... that she'd fallen for Mace in an uncharacteristically love-at-first sight fashion.

But if she could fall in love with someone so fast, certainly she could fall out of love just as easily.

She fervently hoped so.

Zoe Wallace shut the bedroom door, not wanting to hear the man she thought she loved leave.

CHAPTER EIGHT

Mace had his car, so he did something rather unheard of in Hiho…he drove. He drove to Rob Pawley's office. It was only a few blocks from Zoe's. But then, there wasn't much in Hiho that was far from Zoe's.

Right now he felt a lot farther than ten blocks away from her.

And he didn't like it.

He really had planned to tell her about his find in Clover's journal. But last night his mind wasn't on the town's centennial that wasn't.

It was on Zoe. And only on Zoe.

Not just a casual thinking of her, of what it would be like with her, but a total focused, forget-everything-else, sort of way.

Her crack about not knowing him hurt.

Although, he'd be the first to admit that his immediate connection to her was…well, it wasn't like him. Not at all. He wasn't one to trust someone whole-heartedly even after years of knowing them.

He was a reporter. He dealt in facts, not feelings.

And yet, with Zoe there was an immediate spark even the first time he saw her with that horrendous makeover and bobbling eyelash.

Zoe was a beautiful woman, with an astounding capacity for caring … she showed it in the way she dealt with everyone from old *psst*ing reporters, to runaway bulls, to pie-judging concerned old ladies. But more than that, she challenged him. She stood right up to him and argued her points.

This time she was wrong. He truly had intended to tell her what he'd found.

But she'd been right to make him question exactly what he wanted in his career. She'd been right about bigger not always being better.

She was right about being happy.

And being with Zoe made him happy.

So, how was he going to fix … all this?

He mentally made a list.

Fix the centennial-that-wasn't scandal so no one was hurt and he could retain his journalistic integrity.

Fix his career.

And last, but certainly not least, fix things with Zoe, because he suspected he'd never be happy without her. And he'd discovered that she was right when she said that was what mattered.

He pulled up in front of Rob Pawley's, anxious to start solving all the problems he suddenly had.

Rob handed over a copy of the endowment, obviously not thrilled to be doing so. He, like everyone else in town, didn't want to know the truth. But the truth was out there. And if Mace could find it, someone else could, too. So all that was left was to deal with it.

Speaking of dealing with it … it was time for the parade and he still had a story to cover.

He pulled up a few blocks from the parade route, grabbed his camera from the trunk, along with a tripod, and made his way to the Grandstand.

Zoe was sitting up there with a bunch of people. Mace knew he'd met a few of them last night at the party, but after a while their names all ran together.

There was the Mayor, a tiny thing, but a real in-charge sort of lady.

Mace made his obligatory greetings to the crowd as he set up his camera.

Well, he greeted everyone but Zoe, who made it a point of moving out of greeting range. He moved forward, she faded back. He moved toward the back of the crowd, she headed for the side.

How on earth was he going to convince the woman he wasn't a … what had she called him? A fink.

Yeah. That hurt.

Zoe started announcing the parade. "And leading our parade in style, this year, is Joel Carter. Joel is the great-great grandson of our founder, Hiram Hump. Let's give a warm Hiho greeting to Joel."

The crowd clapped wildly.

"And here's Hiho Cloverleaf College's Marching Band with the school mascot, Bessie."

Mace let the tape roll, capturing the parade on film. But try as he might, he couldn't pay attention to the parade. He kept glancing back at the woman announcing.

The woman he'd spent the most amazing night of his life with.

The woman who thought he was a fink.

As Bessie walked right in front a Mace, a bull blundered out onto the parade line from behind the grandstand.

"Jed," Mace muttered.

No one in the crowd was doing anything, not even Zoe, the fearless cowgirl.

Mace sensed a chance to force Zoe to acknowledge him, to look at him. He grabbed a cable that he hadn't needed, but had inadvertently brought for the camera, and fashioned it into a crude lasso, jumped off the grandstand and headed toward the big bull.

The closer he got, the bigger it looked.

Bigger than it had looked when Zoe lassoed it.

Bigger than even Paul Bunyan's Babe.

The thing was a monster.

"Hey, Jed," he crooned, as he approached, lasso ready to go. "Hey, boy."

Mace threw the lasso over the beast's head, reminding himself that Zoe had said the bull was as gentle as a lamb.

As the lasso slid over the bull's neck, Mace suddenly registered that the crowd was quiet.

Not just quiet, they were silent.

But the bull wasn't.

It was snorting.

And it didn't look the least bit lamb-like.

As a matter of fact, it looked annoyed.

Very, very annoyed.

It shook its giant head, then snorted as it charged, right at Mace.

"Mace, it's not Jed," Zoe cried, breaking the silence.

"Oh, no," Mace cried, as he ran, a bull hot on his heels.

The crowd scattered.

Pandemonium ensued.

But the bull-who-wasn't-lamb-like-Jed ignored everything and everyone except Mace.

Mace headed back away from the crowd, toward the back of the town square, knowing that a non-Jed-ish bull could really hurt someone.

He dodged behind trees, keeping one step ahead of the brute.

He ran around a park picnic table. It was big enough to keep the bull from reaching him, and yet small enough that the bull couldn't cut the corners as tight as Mace could, which gave Mace the advantage.

The cord flapped around, uselessly behind the brute.

Suddenly, Mace had an idea.

He sprinted around the table, coming up behind the bull, and grabbed the long cord.

A huge plug that attached the cord to the camera flapped at the end of the line.

As the bull rounded the table, trying to catch Mace, Mace wedged the cord into the space between the picnic table slats.

The bull charged.

The line went taut.

The plug wedged tightly in between the slats and the noose at the end of it pulled tight around the bull's neck—tight enough to stop the beast that was surprised by the weight of the table.

Mace ran out of harms way.

The crowd started clapping wildly.

Mace looked around. He'd forgotten anyone else was there.

Suddenly Zoe was at his side. She slugged him in the arm. "That was a stupid thing to do, Mace Mason."

"Hey, what did you do that for?" He rubbed the spot she'd hit.

"You scared about a decade of life out of me. What were you thinking, chasing after that bull?"

"I thought it was Jed," he muttered, suddenly feeling foolish. He'd wanted to impress Zoe, like some schoolboy doing wheelies on his bike to impress the girls on the playground.

"It wasn't Jed," she assured him.

"I realized that when the beast decided it would be fun to gore me to death."

"If it was Jed, don't you think someone from Hiho would have grabbed it? And didn't you notice that while Jed is a warm cinnamon color, this beast is quite black?"

"No. I just saw a bull heading toward Bessie and thought, *Jed*," he muttered, feeling even more foolish.

"You didn't think and that's why I slugged you. I'm so mad I could slug you again." She raised her hand, looking as if she indeed might slug his shoulder again, but instead she reached out and simply laid it on his arm. "You could have been killed."

"Would you have cared?" he asked softly.

"Of course I'd have cared. If the bull had gored you I would ... it would have ruined the Festival."

Mace thought maybe, just maybe she'd been about to say she'd be upset.

She turned away from him and hollered, "Come on, everyone. Let's get back to the parade so we can get this festival started."

She motioned to a group of men and said, "Fellas, take care of that beast, okay?"

There was a chorus of *sure things* and *you bets* from the group.

"And what about me?" Mace asked.

"You ... you just stay out of harm's way and finish your story."

"Can I see you tonight?" Before she could protest that she'd be too busy, he added, "After the Festival?"

"It's a free country. You can see whoever you want."

"The only one I want to see is you. Please, Zoe, let me explain things."

She sighed. Not a happy girly, *I'm going to see the man I care about* sort of sigh, but a put-upon, *why me?*, sort of one.

Mace didn't care what kind of sigh it was as long as she said yes she'd see him and let him explain.

"Zoe?" he prompted.

"Fine. Ten o'clock. I'll meet you at the fairground's entrance."

"I'll be there."

"Tom Walters, you put those teeth in."

Zoe had a headache that industrial strength aspirin couldn't begin to touch. Runaway bulls, vendors who didn't show up, and finally a pie-judging, toothless man...

And Mace, a quiet thought whispered.

No matter how many other annoying problems dropped in her lap, Mace Mason was the spike pounding in the center of her brain.

"But Zoe, I hate those teeth. They hurt. And I don't need no teeth to taste. I taste just fine without them."

"Zoe," Cora Macintosh said. No, *said* was a generous description. Whined was closer to the truth. "Zoe, you said you'd take care of this. You know he's going to be biased to the cream pies if he's gumming his pie. Gumming nuts doesn't work."

"Speaking of nuts," Tom grumbled.

Zoe was at her wits end. "Tom, either put them in or I'll have to find another judge."

"Then find yourself another judge," he said as he walked away.

"Great, just great," Zoe mumbled, looking over her shoulder as she watched her pie judge walk away.

She spied Mace, a couple tents away, camera raised. He was shooting the crowd. He turned, the camera lens was focused directly on her.

Zoe snapped her head back around so all he could see was her back. She resisted the urge to make a universally known gesture, not because she worried about offending Mace, but because she knew he was perverse enough to leave it in his piece.

"Zoe, now what? The pie judging was supposed to begin at two. Where are you going to find another unbiased, well-toothed man?" Ida asked.

Cora nodded. "Someone who can handle nuts."

Nuts.

That's how Zoe felt.

"What seems to be the problem?" Mace said from behind her.

Slowly Zoe turned around and came face to face with the spike in her brain.

"Nothing you need worry about," she said.

"But maybe I can help," he offered.

"Sure you can, by leaving. Don't you have a story to research?"

"I'm researching even as we speak."

"Good for you." Oh, what a horribly lame retort. Mace Mason had reduced her to the level of a five-year-old. "Now, if you'll excuse us, we have things to see to."

"What sort of things?" Mace asked, obviously not taking her not-so-subtle hints and leaving.

"Well, that Tom—"

"The one with the false teeth?" Mace asked.

"Yes," Cora said. "The false teeth he refuses to wear for the pie judging contest."

Ida nodded. "Zoe told him to wear them or don't judge."

"And he's not judging?" Mace asked.

Zoe nodded and regretted the movement as it aggravated her headache. She must have winced because Mace looked all concerned and asked, "Are you okay?"

"Just a bit of a tension headache," she admitted. "Just the stress of the Festival. I took some aspirin and I'm sure it won't last long."

"Would it help your tension level if I volunteered to judge the pie contest."

"You'd do that?" she asked, feeling surprised that he'd pitch in and help.

"Sure. It'll be a piece of … pie."

"I believe the phrase is piece of cake…" Ida stopped short and laughed. "Oh. You were being funny."

"Not very funny," Zoe muttered, though the two older ladies weren't minding her grumbling. They were practically fawning over Mace.

What was it with this man and women? First Clover, now the Macintosh sisters. Pretty soon he'd have the entire town's female population bowing at his feet.

The entire town … except her.

Oh, she might have been slightly infatuated with him, before she found out he was a ratfink, but now that she knew the truth, she didn't feel the least bit of anything for him.

Nothing.

She watched him work his way through the pies. And finally pronounce Ida and Cora's pie, the winner.

Zoe might have suspected a bias on his part toward the two if she hadn't had their pie before … it deserved to win.

When the crowd in the tent had thinned out, Zoe saw Mace was talking to Clover.

The two walked toward her.

"Thank you for the help, Mace," Zoe said, wishing she didn't sound so stiff, that she could sound as unaffected as she wished she was.

"No problem," he said with that killer grin of his.

A grin that made her forget about where she was momentarily, despite all her good intentions.

"Well, you two go have a good time. I've got to get to the bandstand and make sure that it's all set up for the Larry Morris Trio."

"How's your headache?" Mace asked.

She stopped, surprised that he remembered. "Fine."

"Are you sure?" he asked.

"Sure I'm sure. Don't worry about it. It's not your problem."

He sighed a put-upon, this-woman-is-driving-me-crazy sort of sigh.

Zoe was glad she was driving him insane, because turn about was fair play.

He gave a curt nod and started for the door.

"Zoe, if you're not feeling well, maybe I could help," Clover offered.

"No, really. I'm fine." She smiled at Clover, not wanting her friend to think Zoe minded that she'd been talking to Mace, probably planning another date.

"If you're sure," Clover said.

"Positive."

With obvious reluctance, Clover followed Mace toward the tent-flap.

Mace stopped. "Hey, Zoe, don't forget, ten o'clock."

She'd hoped he would forget, but obviously he hadn't. "Fine," she said.

She breathed a sigh of relief as he left with Clover.

Zoe was glad she had a few peaceful Mace-free hours before she had to meet him.

It was a meeting she wasn't looking forward to.

Not at all.

Mace left the Festival around dinnertime. He let himself into The Herald's office and finally had a chance to study everything he'd accumulated about Hiho's Centennial problems.

He started with the journals Clover had lent him, copying the pertinent sections.

Then he pulled out the copies of the endowment Rob Pawley had given him earlier.

He read through the old document, which was actually short and to the point. The endowment instructions were in a codicil to Pawley's will, instructing that money be set aside and should be awarded to the college and the library upon the town's centennial.

Mace read the document over a number of times, rubbing his temple, wondering if headaches were contagious, because if they were, Zoe had infected him with hers.

He set the paper down and leaned back on the couch, closing his eyes, hoping if he rested them a few minutes, he could will the headache away.

He must have dozed, because he awoke with a start and an idea. A great idea. A brilliant idea.

He reread the codicil.

He had it.

He knew how to fix the centennial thing.

At least he thought he did. He'd have to make some calls and double check his facts, but he was pretty sure he had a way out.

He glanced at his watch.

It was ten-thirty.

Darn.

He was late. Zoe was already upset with him and he didn't think standing her up was going to improve her mood.

He bet she wasn't waiting for him—Zoe wasn't a wait around kind of gal—but just in case, he'd drive by the fairground before heading to her house.

Once he got to her house ... well, he was pretty sure how to fix the Centennial mess, but he'd have to wait and see if he could figure out just what to do with Zoe Wallace.

CHAPTER NINE

Zoe wasn't waiting for him at the fairgrounds.

Mace really hadn't expected she would be there.

So he turned around and headed the few blocks to her house. He was nervous. Acid-eating-away-at-the-lining-of-his-stomach kind of nervous.

He arrived and knocked at her door.

No answer.

She was going to be difficult.

He smiled at the thought. He liked that Zoe could be difficult, that she kept him on his toes, and challenged him at every turn.

He liked the way she laughed.

The way she smiled.

The way she made love to him.

Thinking of making love to Zoe left him wanting to get into her house.

He thumped loudly on the door.

"Zoe, I know you're in there. If you don't open the door I'm going to start to sing. Yes, I'll serenade you, right out here on your porch. Can you imagine the rumors that Loni lady will spread then?"

Still no answer.

He cleared his throat and started, "*Zoe, my lo… ove…*"

The door flew open. "Shh," Zoe told him.

"Are you going to let me in?" he asked with a grin he hoped was endearing.

But Zoe wasn't so easily won over. She glared at him. "No."

He cleared his voice again. *"Zoe, my lo… ove…"*

She grabbed his arm and pulled him into the house, slamming the door behind him.

Mace grinned. "See, I knew you couldn't keep your hands off me."

"What do you want, Mace?"

"I'm sorry I was late," he said, taking a step toward her.

She backed away. "It doesn't matter."

"Yes it does," he took another small step. "I stood you up and I'm sorry. I was working and then fell asleep. You see, I didn't get much sleep last night and was tired."

She blushed. "Well, then you better head to Aunt Aggie's and get some sleep tonight."

She hadn't countered his step with one of her own and Mace felt heartened at the small point. Right now, he'd take whatever he could get.

"I should head to Aunt Aggie's, but I'm not going to. We've got an awful lot to talk about."

"We don't have anything to talk about." She seemed to notice he was closer because she took that step keeping distance between them.

"I'm relieved you think we haven't anything we need to talk about, because I don't want to talk right now."

"You don't?" She took a step backward making the distance between them even wider.

"No." Not willing to have anything separating him from Zoe, he closed the gap.

"If you don't want to talk, why are you here?"

"Because I've been dreaming of doing this all day…" He pulled her into his arms, amazed at how right she felt there. She was a perfect fit.

"Do you know how rare this is?" he murmured as he brushed his lips against her neck.

Zoe stood stiff, not fighting, not pulling away, but not exactly melting in his embrace either.

"Rare? You mean that reporters come to town and accost women?"

"No, this… this thing we have between us. I've dated a lot of women before and I've never felt anything nearly this powerful. It's more than a connection, more than the fact we're both reporters. It's something deeper."

Mace suspected he knew just what it was, but from the look on Zoe's face, she wasn't ready to hear it.

"I want you," he simply said.

"Mace, this can't work. I don't know if I can trust you. You held out information on me."

"Not intentionally. I have so much to tell you and I'm willing to tell you everything you want to know, but I'd like to wait long enough for me to do this…"

No longer willing to wait, he kissed her. For a moment, he thought he'd blown it, but the moment passed and Zoe joined in the kiss, an equal partner.

"I do want those answers and I'm willing to wait a while longer for them. But I'm not willing to wait for other things."

"Like what?" he asked.

"Something bigger and better comes to mind."

She shot him a smile, letting him know that she forgave him, that she knew he wasn't holding out on her.

She believed him.

He gently touched her cheek, awash with something more than desire.

Whether Zoe admitted it or not, they did have something between them, something big, something better than anything he'd ever experienced.

Something that made him very, very happy.

Zoe looked at the man sleeping by her side.

She hadn't got those answers, but it really didn't matter. She trusted Mace.

It was absurd.

She'd been in a big city long enough to know that trusting another reporter was career suicide, but it wasn't Mace-the-reporter she trusted.

It was Mace-the-man.

This man she trusted.

A dark strand of hair tumbled down on his forehead and Zoe gently brushed it back. She wondered how someone she'd known for such a short time could have come to mean so much to her.

How much did he mean?

She knew the answer and was afraid that knowing it was going to make her hurt even more when he left.

Even more was the operative phrase, because she knew she'd miss him as soon as he was gone.

It was Sunday. Their last day together.

Oh, maybe he'd call a few times. Maybe even make the trip down to Hiho from Erie, or whatever bigger and better place he ended up in.

But it wouldn't last.

Long distance relationships never did.

And he hadn't even said he wanted a relationship.

She sighed. She just couldn't unravel the knot she'd gotten herself in.

"What was that sigh for?" Mace asked, his voice husky with sleep.

"Nothing," she said, not willing to voice her concerns and doubts. "Just the sigh of a well-pleasured lady."

"Well pleasured?" he asked, grinning.

"Don't get too conceited there, Mace. For I believe you were a well-pleasured man and you haven't had the good graces to sigh even once this morning."

"If my lady wants a sigh, she'll have one." He drew in a long, exaggerated breath and let it out with excruciating slowness. "There. And I must tell you, that the sigh was only the slightest indication of how truly well pleasured I was."

He reached over and gently touched her hair.

"And though I'd like to see if we could be that well-pleasured again this morning, I'm afraid we don't have time. I'm waiting for a call and have a few things to take care of before this evening's closing ceremonies."

"And we still have to talk," she said.

"Yes, we do."

"Maybe, after the talking and the busy work we have in front of us today we could have one more night before you go?" She worked at keeping her pain at the thought of his leaving out of her voice. She even managed to force a smile.

Mace gave her an odd look that Zoe couldn't even begin to interpret. "After the fireworks tonight, you've got a date."

She let out her breath. She hadn't realized she'd been holding it while she waited for his response. "Good."

"I should probably head over to the Bed and Breakfast for a quick shower and a change of clothes."

Zoe realized how deeply she didn't want him to leave, which made her force an even bigger smile than she'd intended. "That's good."

"I'll meet you back here and bring some of Aunt Aggie's muffins. We can grab a bite while I catch you up on all I've discovered."

She nodded but Mace didn't see her. He was already pulling on his clothes.

He was in an awful hurry to leave.

She had to play it cool, had to convince him that she was okay with him leaving now, and leaving permanently tomorrow morning. That she wasn't emotionally involved in their relationship.

Which meant, she had to do the best acting she'd ever done, because truth be told, she was more than a little emotionally involved with Mace.

She'd lost her heart to him.

She must have been in the shower when the phone rang because the answering machine light was blinking when she got out.

She pushed the message button.

"Zoe, I'm sorry to stand you up again," Mace's voice said over the machine. "I promise to explain everything to you later and you'll know why I couldn't come back this morning. Trust me, okay? I know we haven't known each other long, in terms of days, but Zoe, I feel like I've known you forever. Please, just trust me. I'm trying to see that everything works all right for both of us."

Trust him?

Could she afford to?

He was leaving tomorrow and taking her heart with him. It didn't make any sense, but there you go ... love never made sense. Look at Bessie and Jed.

As much as she wanted to see Mace, to know what was going on, she decided to do as he asked and simply trust him.

Somehow Zoe made it through the longest day of her life. The Festival had a few glitches that kept her running, but on the whole, things went smoothly enough, she thought with a satisfied feeling settling over her. She stood on the grandstand, looking at the people milling all over the fairground.

"*Psst.*"

Bertram.

Just what she didn't need.

"*Psst*, Zoe."

She turned and found him hiding in the shadowed area at the side of the stand.

Feeling like a woman on her way to her executioner, Zoe walked over to him.

"Yes?"

"What did you find?"

"Mace found something. He was going to tell me, but got called away on business."

"You mean, you two had the entire night together and he couldn't find time to share his discovery with you?"

Zoe knew she was blushing as she thought about all they did manage to share last night. "Bertram, that's really none of your business."

"Well, if you feel that way, I'm betting you think it's not anyone in town's business, which is a shame because this town tends to make everyone's business their business. They're all buzzin' about you and your new beau."

"He's not my beau," she said.

She couldn't let the town know how much it was going to hurt her when Mace left. If they were sympathetic, she'd simply drown.

"He's not your beau?" Mace said.

She turned and resisted—barely resisted flinging herself into his arms. Instead she smiled and hoped he could see how glad she was to see him. "Hey, you're back."

"Sorry to stand you up again," he said.

"So what did you find, boy?" Bertram asked.

"I'll tell you all everything later. Right now, I want to talk to Zoe."

"Zoe, Zoe," Pete cried, then he spotted his uncle. "Uncle Bertram, what are you up to?"

"It's okay, boy," Bertram said with a smug look on his face. "They know."

"They know what?" Pete asked slowly.

"They know that Hiho isn't a hundred until next year. Mace here has proof."

Pete sighed. "And I suppose it's too much to hope that you're not going to run with the story."

Mace looked as if he was going to say something but Zoe jumped in first. "Pete, this isn't the type of thing we can keep quiet. The council tried when they took Bertram's proof. But Mace has found more. It's likely that, given enough time and searching, even more evidence will surface. We've got to come clean."

"What about the college?" Pete asked. "Cloverleaf has already borrowed against that money."

"I know and ..." Zoe turned to Mace.

"Do you trust me?" he asked her, watching her with a strange intensity.

"Yes."

If she could fall in love with a man in a week, she certainly knew him well enough to trust him.

Mace turned to Pete and Bertram. "It will all turn out right. It's almost time for the closing ceremonies. Rob Pawley is supposed to present the checks then and you'll see, it will be fine."

"But, but," Pete sputtered.

"What are you up to, boy," Bertram asked.

Mace grinned his self-assured little grin that set Zoe's heart beating proudly.

"It's good, if I do say so myself," he said.

"But—"

"If you'll excuse me, I have to talk to Zoe." He led her away, behind the grandstand.

"Before I say anything, I have to do this..." He kissed her hard and long, as if they'd been away from each other for months, rather than just most of a day.

"Wow," Zoe murmured. "I missed you, too."

"Did you?" he asked, that weird intensity there in his gaze again.

"Yes."

"Zoe, do you believe in fate?"

She shook her head. "No. I've always thought fate was an excuse, something to blame when things didn't work out the way you plan."

"Then how about love-at-first-sight? Do you believe it can happen? You said lust-at-first-sight, but do you believe there can be more than that?"

"I never did before," she answered slowly.

"Before?" he repeated.

"Mace, this last week has taught me about one thing I believe in absolutely...something I never knew existed before this week."

"What's that?" he asked.

"You." She reached out and traced her forefinger down his jawline, marveling at how beautiful he was. "I believe in you, Mace."

"Zoe." His voice was a hoarse whisper.

"It's okay," she said. "You don't have to tell me what you found or what you've got planned. As a reporter I should demand to know, I should be chomping at the bit. But Mace, I believe in you like no one I've ever met before. I trust you."

"But I want to tell you—"

"Zoe," Vicky, the town's mayor, called. "It's time."

"Listen, Mace, I trust that whatever you do is what you feel you have to do."

"Before you go," he said. "I have one thing that can't wait."

"What?"

"I love you."

Chapter Ten

"Wh...wh...what?" Zoe sputtered.

Mace grinned. It wasn't quite the reaction he'd expected, but then, when had Zoe ever done what he expected?

"I asked about love at first sight and fate because, I think that's what this assignment was...fate. And that first time I saw you with that horrendous make-over and that little bobbling eyelash, I think I fell in love with you."

"But, it's been less than a week. That doesn't make sense."

"I don't think time really matters when it comes to the heart. A very wise woman once told me that love's like that, that sometimes there's just nothing you can do to stop it. It will break through any obstacle...even time itself."

He saw that she recognized her own words, the ones she'd used right after she'd lassoed Jed.

He reached out and caressed her cheek. "I've dated a few women a lot longer than a week, and not one has ever made me feel like you do."

"But—"

"I'm not asking you to say the words back," he said. "I'm just asking for a chance, for time to make you see that you love me too."

"How much time will you give me?" she asked.

"As much as you need." Although Mace knew each minute of not knowing would kill him.

"Well, now, it could take a bit of time." Zoe glanced at her watch.

"Like I said—"

"Zoe," Vicky yelled.

"Mace, I've got to go. The closing ceremony is about to start and I have to be there."

"Go. We'll talk after."

She started running toward the grandstand, then stopped and turned around. "About how much time I need. I'd had enough before you finished speaking. I love you, too." She turned around and fled.

Mace watched the woman he loved head onto the stage, surprised to hear those three words so soon. He figured it would take a lot longer…at least until after the Festival.

But that was Zoe, always surprising him.

He smiled. Well, she had a few surprises coming her way.

"…and now, I'd like to introduce—not that he needs an introduction—Rob Pawley."

Rob came out on stage carrying two huge checks. He walked up to the microphone and said, "Citizens of Hiho. It's come to my attention that we have a slight problem. You see, although we've always been told that the town was founded in May of 1918, it has been discovered that due to a clerical error, the town wasn't actually officially a town until February 1919."

A murmur ruffled through the crowd.

Zoe saw Cloverleaf's President Stanley and Katy Sloane both wince and she felt horrible for them. The library could probably limp by another year, but the college was counting on that money, having already borrowed against it.

Rob held up his hand. "Let me read to you the actual wording of the endowment. '…the endowments to be presented to the Hiho Public Library and Cloverleaf College when the community celebrates its Centennial.' As I said, there is now proof that this year is not our Centennial."

The crowd was muttering now. Loudly.

People were obviously upset.

Zoe sympathized. She was upset as well, but she didn't blame Mace. He'd done what he needed to do, what any good journalist would do—he'd told the story.

"But," Rob was saying, "Hiho's newest resident, Mace Mason, a documentary film-maker for the History Channel, pointed out that the Pawley endowment was to be awarded when the town *celebrated* its Centennial. And thanks to our own Zoe Wallace, I think this Festival counts as one of the best celebrations I've ever seen. What do you think?"

The crowd roared its approval.

Zoe registered the fact that the endowments were saved, but she was more focused on what else Rob had said. *Newest resident? History Channel?*

Zoe scanned the crowd, searching for Mace as Rob presented the endowment checks to Katy Sloane from the library and Cloverleaf's President, Leonard J. Stanley.

Where was he?

"*Psst,* Zoe," Bertram said, from off-stage.

"You heard?" she said, still looking for Mace.

"Yeah. He's a smart one, that boy is. But it's not about that. There are a few of the college students over behind the stables and it looks like they're up to something. I've been a reporter too many years not to know when something's up and something's definitely up with those boys. They're—"

"Zoe, will you come here please?" Rob asked, beckoning her to the microphone.

"I'll check it out as soon as I'm done here," she stage-whispered as she rose and walked to the microphone.

Vicky was back at the microphone. "Zoe, on behalf of the entire community, I want to thank you for the wonderful job you did coordinating this festival."

"Thank you, Mayor Robertson. It was my pleasure."

She turned to go back to her seat, but Vicky said, "Before you go, there's one more thing..."

Zoe turned back and walked to the mic. Mace came out of the far wing and walked up to the microphone.

"I just want to thank everyone for all their help this week as I worked on my piece about Hiho for WMAC news in Erie. I'm sorry to report it's the last piece I'll be doing for WMAC because I've turned in my resignation."

"Mace?" Zoe whispered.

Rob's comment about Mace being Hiho's newest citizen sank in. Her heart felt as if it were going to beat out of her chest.

"You see, someone I care about told me that I'd been chasing a fool's dream. I thought that I wanted bigger and better things in my career, but I've found this person was right... happy is what matters the most. So, I've taken a position doing a documentary series on obscure figures in history for The History Channel. The new position allows me a great deal of freedom in choosing where I live, and I choose..."

He paused and smiled at Zoe.

"I choose Hiho, Ohio. At least I do if Zoe will agree to consider marrying me."

The crowd screamed so loud that Zoe wasn't sure Mace could even hear her as she flung herself into his arms and whispered, "Yes."

But his whoop of happiness told her he had.

They left the microphone and Vicky stepped back up. "And now, to close out this Centennial-that-wasn't Celebration, let me present the Cloverleaf marching band and our fireworks.

Explosions of light lit the sky, as the band played Hiho's town song. In the back of her mind, Zoe realized that it sounded much better without the words.

But that was way in the back of her mind.

In the forefront was a sense of wonder and awe that she was being held by the man she loved … a man who loved her back.

A man who'd learned that happiness mattered.

"Zoe," Bertram hollered, no *psst* at all this time, just a horrendous sense of urgency. "Those boys—"

Suddenly there was a huge bang overhead from a much closer distance than the fireworks.

Much, much closer.

A fine dust sprinkled down on the crowd and suddenly …

Zoe itched everywhere she had bare skin. She wasn't the only one. Everyone in her vicinity was scratching.

The firework display continued, but the band had stopped and was scratching as well.

"—those boys shot off itching powder in some home-made rockets," Bertram finished. "I got Sheriff Smith, but it was too late."

Zoe groaned as she scratched.

Mace laughed.

"You know, when I gave my life a makeover and decided to move here, I thought a small town would be boring, but with mysterious centennials-that-aren't, runaway bulls and itching powder … well, let's just say it's a bit more exciting than I anticipated." He grabbed her and pulled her into his arms. "And with the woman I love in it, it's the most exciting place on earth."

"I love you, too," Zoe said, mid-scratch. "But I think we better get home and shower this stuff off."

"And then?"

"And then we'll talk about fate, about love at first sight… about us."

"Sounds just about right to me," Mace said.

The following week's Hiho Herald's front page headline read, THE CENTENNIAL THAT WASN'T. The two other headlines proclaimed, FORMER ERIE REPORTER FINDS A SOLUTION and finally LOCAL PAPER OWNER, ZOE WALLACE IS ITCHING TO TIE THE KNOT WITH HISTORY CHANNEL'S NEWEST DOCUMENTARY PRODUCER, MACE MASON.

EPILOGUE

"*Hiho, Ohio, a quiet, lovely town. Hiho, Ohio, where no one wears a frown…*" the chorus sang. Thankfully the crowd's applause drowned out the last few bars of the song, saving Zoe's ears.

She stepped forward on the stage of the college's new theater and stared out at the audience and smiled.

"Welcome to Hiho, Ohio's *Second Annual* Centennial Celebration," she said into the microphone. The crowd once again applauded wildly.

It was bigger than last year's crowd. The whole Centennial-That-Wasn't story that Mace put together for WMAC had been picked up on a national level.

Six month's later, his documentary on Hiram Hump had aired on the History Channel. His documentary series, *Hazy History*, was doing well. He'd leave town for a week or two at a time, but he always came back home.

Home to Hiho.

Home to Zoe.

"And now, let me introduce our Mayor."

Zoe stepped back as Vicky took center-stage and started speaking.

Two arms wrapped around her and Zoe leaned into her husband's chest, his hands resting on her slightly rounded stomach.

"How are you feeling," he whispered in her ear, his breath tickling against her neck.

She turned and smiled at Mace, "Fine. We're both fine. You don't have to worry."

"Ah, but worry is what we husbands do best."

"Mace, do you remember what you asked me here last year?"

"What?"

"You asked if I believed in fate and in love at first sight."

Those words were etched in her mind as some of the sweetest she'd ever heard. How on earth had she got so lucky?

She thought she was happy when she left New York and settled in Hiho, but how she felt then couldn't even begin to compare to the amount of happiness she felt now. It was bone deep and so strong it occasionally took her breath away with its intensity.

"When I asked you, you said no you didn't believe in love at first sight or in fate."

"I said no I didn't believe in them ... but I believed in you. I still do. So go knock them dead." She kissed his cheek even as Vicky said, "And now, I'd like to introduce Hiho's resident historian, Mace Mason."

He stepped up to the microphone. "A year ago, I came to Hiho to do a small piece on its centennial and a short documentary on Hiram Hump for my station, WMAC. And here I am, a year later, and I've given my life a makeover. I'm a resident of Hiho and about to unveil my newest installment for *Hazy History* called, Hiho, Ohio and the Centennial-That-Wasn't."

He stepped back and the theater darkened as the screen lit up and Mace's voice narrated, "Someone once told me that bigger wasn't necessarily better, that happy was. Here in a lazy little town in central Ohio, happy seems to be the name of the game …"

Mace came back to Zoe and sat next to her.

And at that moment, during Hiho, Ohio's Second Annual Centennial Celebration, Zoe Wallace Mason sat next to her husband, her hand resting on her unborn child and knew that happy didn't even begin to describe her life.

Dear Reader,

After I wrote *Not Precisely Pregnant* I knew I wanted to do another reporter story. So I sent Mace to cover a small town celebration. Writing a fluff piece about a small town in the middle of nowhere rankles. Mace doesn't realize he's met his match in Zoe. I had so much fun taking a classic opposites-attract story and adding in horrible makeovers, lovesick cattle and a town secret. I hope you enjoyed your visit to Hiho, Ohio. If you did, please leave a review and help other readers discover *The Makeover*.

As always, thank you for all your support!

Holly